ACCIDENTAL
FRIENDS

★

Helena Pielichaty
ACCIDENTAL
FRIENDS

OXFORD
UNIVERSITY PRESS

OXFORD
UNIVERSITY PRESS

Great Clarendon Street, Oxford OX2 6DP

Oxford University Press is a department of the University of Oxford.
It furthers the University's objective of excellence in research, scholarship,
and education by publishing worldwide in

Oxford   New York

Auckland   Cape Town   Dar es Salaam   Hong Kong   Karachi
Kuala Lumpur   Madrid   Melbourne   Mexico City   Nairobi
New Delhi   Shanghai   Taipei   Toronto

With offices in

Argentina   Austria   Brazil   Chile   Czech Republic   France   Greece
Guatemala   Hungary   Italy   Japan   Poland   Portugal   Singapore
South Korea   Switzerland   Thailand   Turkey   Ukraine   Vietnam

Oxford is a registered trade mark of Oxford University Press
in the UK and in certain other countries

British Library Cataloguing in Publication Data

Data available

ISBN: 978-0-19-275510-0

1 3 5 7 9 10 8 6 4 2

Printed in Great Britain by Cox and Wyman Ltd, Reading, Berkshire

Paper used in the production of this book is a natural, recyclable product made
from wood grown in sustainable forests. The manufacturing process conforms
to the environmental regulations of the country of origin.

For Peter
with all my love

EMMA AND KAZIA

The loud rattling startled Emma, making her step back and bang her heel into the ladder. Wincing, she turned and saw the rattling was coming from one of the college cleaners' trolleys as it rode over the low step leading through to Art Studio One. Realizing that it was that time already—the studios were always last to be cleaned as they took the longest—only added to Emma's mounting despair. Her exhibition was nowhere near finished. Not only that, it was a pathetic load of rubbish the examiners would take one look at in the morning and rip to shreds. Fact.

OK, so her tutor, Phil Kiddey, had assured her that she had absolutely nothing to worry about. That she was, according to him, not rubbish at all but actually a 'bit of a superstar'. Emma let out a heavy sigh. The trouble with Phil was he always said stuff like that, not just to her but to all the students on his course. Everyone was a 'star' and everything they did was either 'marvellous' or 'stunning' or 'innovative'. What she could do with was a second opinion from someone who would see her exhibition with a fresh, objective eye. Someone who didn't know her. Someone like . . .

1

Emma looked again at the cleaner. The woman had her back to her, her thin shoulder blades jutting through the sheer material of her tabard like set squares, her dark head bent as she selected her cleaning materials ready to begin. Emma recognized her instantly. It was the Polish one who had started soon after Christmas and caused a furore by mistakenly chucking away two students' sculptures that had been left propped against the waste bins to dry. She'll be perfect, Emma thought to herself. Impulsively, she strode across the floor and touched the cleaner lightly on the arm. 'Excuse me.'

The woman, just as startled by Emma as Emma had been by her moments earlier, knocked over a can of Mr Sheen as she glanced round.

'I'm sorry, I didn't mean to make you jump,' Emma said, righting the can and trying to read the name on the badge pinned to the cleaner's breast. 'Er . . . Kaz-ia . . . '

'Not Kazz. Is pronounced Kasha to rhyme with smasher,' the woman explained, in clear, if heavily accented, English.

'Oh! Well, nice to meet you, Kazia . . . I'm Emma,' Emma said and held out her hand for the woman to shake.

The cleaner stared at it, puzzled. She was not used to the students speaking directly to her, let alone offering actual physical contact. Emma continued quickly. 'I was wondering if you'd help me? I've been stressing over my exhibition for so long I'm going cross-eyed.'

'Help you? But I have room to clean,' Kazia pointed out, pulling on a pair of yellow rubber gloves.

Emma nodded to show she understood. 'Oh, don't worry; I'll help you with that, I promise. I just want a second opinion on something.'

At once the cleaner looked interested. She even smiled, revealing white, if slightly crooked, teeth. 'Like Dr Grey!' she beamed.

'Sorry?' Emma asked.

'In excellent TV hospital drama called Grey's Anatomy, Doctor Meredith Grey often asks her handsome but married ex-lover Doctor Derek Shepherd for a second opinion, though she does not always take it, silly woman.'

'Oh, right,' said Emma, 'my mum watches that. She's a big fan.'

'Did she see the one where Meredith had to keep her fist inside the man's chest because there was a bomb there and if she moves even a millimetre the whole hospital blows up?'

'Er . . . I don't know.'

'It was so exciting. I daren't breathe for whole episode.'

'Really? Wow. I'll try and catch it on DVD.'

'You should,' Kazia said, her eyes swooping over Emma from head to toe, the way one human does to another: assessing, judging, instinctively compartmentalizing. Kazia saw a brown-skinned young woman with a pretty face framed by a mass of curly, coppery coloured hair, her slim, petite frame drowning in a paint-splattered boilersuit. The girl also had bare feet, which Kazia found endearing, if a little rash in this particular room. Who knew what you could tread on in here? Plaster. Staples. Glue. Oh, well—art students were strange like that; it was not her business. 'OK,' Kazia agreed, beginning to peel off her gloves, 'I will give you second opinion. Show me but quickly, yes? Or I will have big behind.'

'Five minutes max, I promise!' Emma laughed, leading her over to the far wall where her four canvases, each about the size of a ping-pong table, dominated the space. 'What I'd really love is if you'd walk along each panel with me so I can practise what I'm going to say to the examiners tomorrow. They're assessing me at ten and I am so nervous.'

'I understand,' Kazia nodded. 'Day before my driving test I was on toilet non-stop.'

Emma hurriedly filed that snippet away under 'too much information' and continued. 'O-K. If you'll just stand over here for a minute, I'll give you a brief introduction.' Emma manoeuvred Kazia so that she was standing adjacent to the panels, then cleared her throat and began the opening speech she had prepared during lunch. 'The concept of my work is based upon my first year here at Hercules Clay Further Education College, two years ago. Using the game of Consequences, I hope to demonstrate the sequence of events as they unfolded through a variety of techniques and media . . . '

Kazia interrupted then. 'Oh. You are on a three-year course? I did not know there was a three-year art and design course here.'

'There isn't. I took a year out.'

'Oh. Why?'

The question threw Emma off guard. The examiners wouldn't want to know about that, would they? It was too personal. And certainly too personal to talk to a virtual stranger about. 'Er . . . well, I think that's kind of irrelevant at the moment. Anyway, Consequences,' she continued, ' . . . although this might seem like a children's game, in actual fact it . . . '

Kazia interrupted again. 'I do not think we had this game when I was growing up in Wroclaw. Could you explain it, please?'

'You've never played it?'

'No,' Kazia said.

Emma gawped in astonishment. Until now she had presumed everybody had heard of Consequences. What if the examiners hadn't heard of it either? Maybe it was only her family who sat round the table on rainy Saturday afternoons and made up silly stories on scraps of paper. Nightmare! She'd failed from the out-set! These were basics she should have predicted! Oh, crap!

Frantically, Emma ripped a sheet of paper from the spiral bound book she had been using to jot notes down. 'OK, I'll explain it to you. It's dead easy. What you do is take a piece of paper like this. Then you have to write down a boy's name on top. I'll write my brother Dan's down because it's short . . . ' Quickly, Emma printed 'Dan' in neat capital letters. 'Then you fold the paper over to cover it, like this.'

Kazia watched intently. 'Mmm.'

'Then you write a girl's name. Do you want to do the girl's name?' Emma held out the pen but Kazia shook her head.

'I have terrible handwriting. Like drunken carp. You do it for me,' she said.

'What shall I write? I could put Becky? That's my sister. Nine going on nineteen, unlike Dan who's twenty going on twelve.'

'Not Becky. I like name Meredith better,' Kazia said, 'no offence to sister.'

'None taken.' Emma wrote Meredith with a flourish then folded the piece of paper over as before. 'So that's the first part.'

'OK,' Kazia nodded, 'you were right. Dead easy.'

'Indeed,' Emma said, calming down a little. 'Now, this piece of paper links neatly with my first piece of art which, as you can see from the label on the wall, is entitled "Consequences Part One: Boy's Name/Girl's Name".' Emma paused, waiting until Kazia had slipped the paper into her pocket and turned to face the panel.

They stood for a few seconds, Kazia to take in the work for the first time, Emma for the millionth. 'This represents my typographical element,' Emma added.

Kazia studied the abstract design intently. It consisted of repeating four short names, James, Grace, Leon, and Emma time and again in different colours, shapes, and sizes, vertically, horizontally, diagonally; sometimes separate, sometimes overlapping. Sometimes the names were painted, sometimes printed, other times filled with cut-out bits of newspapers or letters or documents. 'These are the names of your friends? James, Grace, and Leon?' Kazia asked.

Emma nodded. 'Yes. They are the first people I met here, on day one.'

'Ah,' Kazia replied. 'The people you meet first are often the ones you stick to.'

'I guess.'

Kazia sniffed and then took a deep breath. 'Well, I like the way you have used a wide variety of typefaces with serifs and sans-serifs,' she said slowly, then added, 'Good use of colour too. Strong colours but one does not dominate the other.'

Emma stared at her. 'You know about serifs?'

Kazia nodded and looked most pleased with herself. 'Mr Kiddey is very kind. He lends me lots of books on art so I can learn what is garbage and what is not garbage when I am cleaning studio.'

'Oh.'

'So it is nice for me to be asked by student to give second opinion. I can use my knowledge.' Kazia smiled then stepped forward and examined a large letter J. 'What is the significance of the print inside here?'

Yes, Emma thought to herself; this was exactly the type of question she could expect! She flicked her hair back from her shoulders in preparation for her answer. 'What you see are scans of our GCSE results. I've used them in all the letters, where appropriate. Basically Consequences is all about the consequences of what happened to the four of us on the day the results were

announced. It was because of them—or lack of them—
we all met that September. I wanted to explore the
effect a common rite of passage, such as the taking of
GCSEs, could have on four random individuals.'
Emma glanced anxiously at Kazia. Had she sounded
too pretentious?

Kazia simply nodded, then leaned even closer to
read the print inside the J. 'So, this James. He was
bright boy?'

At the mention of James's name, Emma felt the back
of her neck warming. 'Very bright,' she agreed.

'So the consequences for him were good?' Kazia
asked, wanting to sound keen and interested.

'Erm . . . no, actually, they weren't. Not really.
Not . . . immediately anyway.'

Kazia frowned. Even though she didn't know very
much about GCSEs the grades given in the large 'J'
looked reasonable to her. 'Please explain more.'

'About why I chose those particular typefaces?'

'No. About why James did not have good consequences with his grades.'

'Oh,' Emma said, hesitating. This was the third
thing she hadn't anticipated: that she'd be asked questions on the personalities behind her letters. She could
have understood it if she'd been doing portraiture.
Hadn't Tracy Chevalier written a whole book about a
maid in one of Vermeer's paintings? Girl with a Pearl
Earring or something? But for an abstract design
piece? Would she be expected to talk about the people behind that? Yet why not? That's what made art

8

interesting, wasn't it? Gave it depth? Brought it to life? Who knew what the examiners would ask! Phil warned they'd throw in the odd curved ball; maybe this would be one. 'Well, OK. Er . . . to understand about the impact of James's results, you have to go back three years, to a Thursday in late August, and imagine you are in a very old boys' public school in West Sussex . . . '

'Like Eton? With cricket and rugger and midnight feastings?'

Emma smiled. 'Well, not Eton exactly but yes, along those lines.'

Kazia nodded enthusiastically. She approved whole-heartedly of public schools, along with all other things British like Yorkshire pudding and Pears' soap and haggis. 'Go on,' she urged.

Emma rubbed her neck and stared once more at the swooping letter J on her panel. 'If I remember from what he told me, James opened his results in the library . . . '

BOY'S NAME: JAMES

In the recesses of an oak-panelled window seat, two boys sat opposite each other, their backs against either side of the wooden shutters, their knees raised in harmonious peaks.

The boy on the left was small for his age with fair hair and skin freckled from a recent holiday in the Mediterranean. He grinned as he handed back a sheaf of papers to the other boy. 'Get bent, Glenfield, you must think I'm a complete tool! Now show me your real ones!' he told his friend, booting him in the shin for good measure.

The other boy, James, his skin not nearly as tanned but still with a healthy glow from participating in outdoor pursuits with the other boarders who stayed on during the holidays, took the sheets, prodding them deep into his blazer pocket. He, too, managed a grin, despite the unexpected waves of nausea swamping his guts. 'These are the real ones, you knob. You owe me fifty quid, as promised. I accept all major credit cards.'

Quinny snorted. 'You lying toad! No way did you get eight Ds.' Alongside most of the year, James had been predicted straight As.

James turned to look out of the window. Below, on the narrow path leading to the main entrance, parents' cars continued to arrive and depart, as they had been doing all morning, with monotonous regularity. 'I know. I ballsed up. I was aiming for Es. And I can't tell you how gutted I am about the A and three Bs.'

For the first time, Quinny wondered whether James might possibly be telling the truth. 'James, you're not saying you actually went through with the bet? You weren't serious?'

James smiled wryly. 'I did and I was. I *told* you I was!'

'Christ on a snowboard!' Quinny exclaimed and demanded a second inspection of the papers. He handed them back with a shake of his head. 'Just because of what Machin said?' he asked.

'Just because of what Machin said,' James acknowledged.

Machin was their maths tutor, who, last January, had ridiculed them all for struggling with Probability. 'For goodness' sake, you morons!' he'd scoffed. 'GCSEs have been dumbed down so much even kids in sink schools can get A stars! Your privileged little hides should be able to pass them in your sleep.'

Machin's assertion had stuck with James. He'd told Quinny he was going to test Machin out by attending lessons and doing the basics for the rest of Year Eleven but nothing else. No wider reading, no extra prep, no revision.

'Fifty notes says you will cram like the rest of us,' Quinny had wagered.

'Fifty notes says I won't.'

Back in the present, Quinny frowned as he realized something. 'James! You didn't get five A to Cs!'

'Correct.'

'That means you won't be able to stay on for the Sixth, you dumb scrote.'

James dismissed that idea with a shrug. 'Come on! I'll just have to do re-sits in November that's all. No sweat.'

'Will your mother let you?'

James continued to stare out of the window. 'Of course she will! She's not going to actually have me live with her, is she? Haven't you seen her website? She's an extremely busy person running that highly successful antiques business in Dubai. You can't expect the poor woman to be a parent as well as a money-making machine, can you?'

Quinny, remembering the number of parents' evenings, sports events, and drama productions Mrs Glenfield had missed over the years, knew that James's cynicism was well-founded and moved on to brighter things. 'What did your dad say? Does he know?'

James held out the text message his father had sent him from LA an hour ago. It read: 'An A without revising. Genius!'

Quinny laughed. 'Your dad is so laid back. It must be the gay thing.'

'Yeah. Must be,' James replied but he couldn't help thinking his dad, gay or not, would have been even more 'laid back' if he'd send him his maintenance now and again. Relying on his mother for all things financial made James feel too beholden. She used every opportunity to remind him of how much he was costing her. As if on cue to remind him again, the sound of gravel being sprayed at high speed heralded her arrival.

Both boys peered down as an open-topped black Lexus sport coupé pulled up on the lawned area perilously close to a stone urn. Quinny whistled. 'Ooh! Close but no cigar! Better luck next time, Mrs G.'

James said nothing as his mother slid elegantly and unhurriedly out of the car, readjusted her sunglasses, and sashayed out of sight towards the main entrance.

Some hours later, Carolyn Glenfield's demeanour was far less poised. 'A bet!' she repeated for the umpteenth time, as she paced once more along the length of the carpet in her hotel room. 'A bet!'

James, slumped in a deep-sided bucket chair by her bed, wearily tried to explain everything again. 'Look, Mum, I know you're hacked off with me but I can take re-sits. I can even do the Fifth again if I have to. I'll make an effort this time, I promise.'

Carolyn stopped dead and shot him a look so withering the room temperature plummeted fifteen degrees then she walked abruptly over to the mini-bar where she began rummaging among the doll-sized bottles and miniature cans. She poured herself a gin and tonic and downed it in one before turning her attention back to her son. 'James, tell me something. Do you think *I'm* a moron?'

'Course not,' James sighed.

'Then where on earth do you get the notion that I'll be spending one more penny on your education?'

'What do you mean?'

Carolyn's eyes were ice hard. 'I mean that seeing that you are so keen not to be seen as privileged you can go without privilege, like I had to when I was your age. Tomorrow, instead of coming back with me to Dubai for the rest of the summer holidays as planned, I'll be driving you to Imogen's . . .'

'Imogen's?' James spluttered. 'I'm not going to Imogen's. No way!'

He had managed to avoid seeing his toxic elder sister for years and didn't see why he should start now. His mother, however, ignored his protest. 'She's just moved into a house I've bought as an investment in the East Midlands. Bay Tree House. It's in a village called Collingham near Newark; convenient for one of the antiques fairs I scout round every now and then. Immie's going to run her interior design business from there. You can live with her for a year. Heaven knows I've lent her enough money I'll never see again; she can pay some back in your keep.'

James felt his throat contract, as if someone were choking him. Of all the scenarios he'd envisaged, this hadn't been one of them. 'Mum, please. You know Imogen hates me. You can't just uproot me from all I've known and pack me off to her like some asylum seeker!'

Carolyn's mouth twisted into a thin, malicious curve. 'Want to bet?' she asked.

'Oh dear, this is not so good start for James,' Kazia said, shaking her head.

'No,' Emma agreed.

Kazia thought she detected something in Emma's voice, a hint of regret? Even sadness? Not wanting to seem over-inquisitive, she didn't probe further. Instead she pointed to a beautifully rounded G in the centre of the panel. 'What about this one, this G for Grace? Did she have better news on GCSE day? Did she try hard?' Kazia's eyes roamed from the rounded G to other Gs; the ones encompassing the scanned results.

'Oh yes, Grace tried hard,' Emma told her.

'Good. Tell me about the day she got her results.'

'Have you got time?'

'Of course. I am very interested.'

'OK,' Emma agreed. In for a penny, in for a pound, she thought. 'It's the same day in August but a bit closer to home. About half a mile from where we are now, in fact. Just up Bowbridge Road . . . '

'Ah! I know it. Near the hospital.'

'Yes,' Emma nodded, 'near the hospital . . . '

GIRL'S NAME: GRACE

Grace Healey lifted the hem of her baggy Notts County shirt and tucked her envelope into her back pocket. Unlike the rest of her year, ripping their results open so publicly and having the screaming abdabs in the school hall, she had promised her mother Aileen she would wait and open them with her. That meant either hanging on until her mother's shift at Hawton's finished at six or walking round to the shop now. Grace knew there was no way she could hang on until six but she had four-year-old Darius with her today and she didn't like mixing business with personal stuff. Still, this was a special occasion; she could break her own strict rules on babysitting for once, she decided. Behind her, she heard Melissa Fitzsimmons squeal at the top of her voice, 'Oh my God! I got three As! Oh my God! Three As!' Daft tart.

Grace reached down and took Darius's warm hand in hers. 'Come on, Darius, let's scram,' she said.

Darius took a bite of his banana and nodded in agreement.

Hawton's Convenience store on Bowbridge Road was half a mile from the school but Darius's love of patting all things furry plus the added bonus of a dead hedgehog in the roadside meant the journey took twice as long as it should have. Grace didn't mind. She was growing more and more nervous about her results. She needed a D and an E to do the Level Two Childcare Course at Hercules Clay College. Childcare was all she'd ever wanted to do, since she was twelve and had first started babysitting and discovered kids loved her as much as she loved them. The course would give her proper qualifications and then, after a bit of experience in nurseries and playschools, she'd set up her own nursery looking after children with special needs. *But* she needed the D and the E to kickstart everything and the stern-faced woman who had interviewed her—Mrs Fletcher, head of faculty—had emphasized she wouldn't be allowed on without them. What if she'd failed? She was no Melissa Fitzsimmons when it came to schoolwork, that was for sure. As they walked, Grace felt her stomach knotting tighter and tighter.

Eventually they reached the shop and Grace nervously pushed open the door for Darius to enter. Like most convenience stores, Hawton's contained more goods than it had room for and felt squashed with more than three people in it. Today was jam-packed. Too late Grace realized it was giro day and turned straight back round, intending to return later, but she had forgotten her mother's uncanny ability to see through tins.

'Grace! Grace!' Aileen called across the aisles from the counter, waving her plump arms around in the air.

'Busted,' Grace said to Darius.

'Busted,' Darius repeated.

Grace pushed her way through the queue of people waiting to pay and stood by the Fruitibix display at the counter.

Mrs Sergeant, an octogenarian with alopecia who had been about to ask for her sixty Benson and Hedges, turned to Grace. 'Oh, speak of the devil! I timed that well! Open 'em then, duck. We can't wait.'

Grace's eyes slid from Mrs Sergeant's to her mother's. 'Mam!' Grace remonstrated.

Aileen patted her pillar-box red hair and looked unwaveringly back at her only child. 'What?' she asked.

'You didn't have to tell everyone!'

'Course I did. This is a big day for me and your dad. You'll be the first one in the family ever to go to college. We're dead proud of you.' Someone in the queue said 'Aww.'

'I haven't got in yet,' Grace mumbled, turning pink.

Her mother dismissed her concerns in an instant. 'Oh, you will have! The amount of time you spent revising! I couldn't get a word out of you for three weeks. Now open the thing before I do!'

She would, too, knowing her, Grace thought. She sighed and pulled the envelope out from her jeans' pocket. It felt warm and smooth. She dug her thumbnail into the sealed edge and tore roughly along it, hanging her head so that her long, thin hair hung in ragged tendrils and obscured her face. A hush seemed to fall on the shop then. Everyone waited. Darius, sensing something was occurring, wrapped his arms round his babysitter's leg and burped.

Grace read slowly, double-checking the figures twice before a grin broke out on her face. English Language E, childcare D, maths E, food technology D, the rest Fs. 'I've done it!' she told her mum. 'I've done it!'

Aileen Healey let out a shriek and immediately heaved herself through the small gap between the tobacco section and the counter, sending the display of Fruitibix crashing to the floor. She trampled over the cereal boxes to get to Grace and gave her a bone-crunching hug. Somewhere below, Darius clung on to Grace's leg for dear life. 'You star!' Aileen shouted. 'I am so proud of you! After all you've been through! Oh, give us a kiss, you brainy little bugger!'

Grace decided she didn't care what anybody thought and she planted a whopper on her mum's wobbly cheek. This was, after all, the happiest moment of her life.

Kazia clapped her hands together in delight. 'Oh, I like this story! G for Grace. Her mum gave her big cuddle.'

'Yes; her mum's a cuddler all right!' Emma smiled.

'Even though her grades were not so good as James's, I think?'

'They were good for Grace; that's all that mattered.'

'I think I am a little like Grace. My school grades not so good, either. Head in clouds, my teachers always telling me.'

'Aw,' Emma said, 'there's nothing wrong with being a dreamer.'

The cleaner took out a handkerchief from her pocket and blew hard into it, wiping her nose with a flourish when she had finished. 'Huh! Try tell Mr Novaki that!' she said, then nodded towards the typography on the wall. ' OK. L for Leon. Tell me about him. He got fine GCSEs?'

'Leon? No. He didn't get any.'

'Not any? Goodness! Where was he on day of results then?'

'In court.'

BOY'S NAME: LEON

The grey-haired magistrate whispered something to the woman next to him. They both nodded gravely before the magistrate looked up and fixed his eyes on the slightly built, fidgety fifteen-year-old boy before him. 'Fazal Mahmood. Although we have taken all mitigating circumstances into account, the fact remains you were responsible for starting a fire which resulted in extensive damage to the science block of Carlton Hill School in May of this year . . . '

Fazal dipped his head slightly. 'S right. He did. Went up like a rocket. Who'd have thought it with that puny amount of petrol they'd used? 'mazin'!

'Not only that, you blatantly waved an imitation fire-arm at the cameras as you carried out your crime . . . '

A tiny smirk this time. 'S right. He did. That'll show that divvy headmaster not to exclude his mates a month before their exams for doing fuck-all wrong. Didn't matter for him, like. He could barely read and write so it made no difference but for his mates it was harsh and disrespectful and nobody dissed his mates, see.

' . . . For the crime of arson and possession of a

replica firearm the court sentences you to twelve months' custody in Briarswood Youth Offenders Centre of which you must serve a minimum of four months.'

Fazal stuck his thumb in the air and grinned at the magistrate. 'Thanks, mush. I'll send you a postcard,' he replied cheerfully. He was careful not to look across to where his mother and uncles were sitting. He took great pains to block out the sound of his mother's sobs and cries of 'No, No.' He didn't want to know about stuff like that. Instead he focused on Leon, his right-hand man, his Numero Duo, and winked as he was led away. 'See you in a mo, geezer! I'll save you a seat in the sweatbox!'

Across the room, Leon nodded, certain that he would. He felt his palms moisten as the magistrates' bench turned their attention to him. The starchy shirt collar round his neck felt tight and constricting and he hated the strangled feel it gave him. At the same time his social worker, Mrs Sadiqi, nudged him to stand up. He did so, slowly rising and unfurling, like a tall, slender-stemmed, black amaryllis.

The magistrate focused on him now, peering over his half-rimmed specs and frowning. 'Leon Jeremiah Wilford. You have admitted aiding and abetting this crime. However, witnesses have testified to seeing you attempt to put out the fire and I am satisfied you were not in the possession of any sort of weapon. Taking into account your previously unblemished record and good reports from some of the teachers at your school, the behavioural unit, and your social worker who testify to you being bright but slightly naive and easily led . . . '

Leon shot Mrs Sadiqi a dirty look and clenched his jaw tight. They'd made him sound like a right little sucker-boy.

' . . . we feel a custodial sentence would not be appropriate in this instance. There is a new scheme being trialled by the region's Youth Offenders Programme for which we think you will be suitable. It is called Fresh Start and is based in Newark. Therefore you will be given a twelve month Suspension Order but you will serve it under the guidelines set out under the scheme . . . ' The magistrate then began blathering on about curfews and conditions. Leon wasn't listening. Inside his head it felt as if his brain were short-circuiting. Thousands of tiny wires were making zzt-zzt-zzt sounds as he stared blankly at the empty space where Faz had been. This was unreal. He was meant to be with Fazal. He was meant to get sent down too. What were the idiots all playing at?

Kazia nodded. 'I see. That explains why the Ls in his name are empty?'

'That's one reason I left them blank,' Emma admitted, 'but also when I first met Leon, well, he just seemed kind of empty and confused.'

'To want to go to jail he must have been confused!'

'Exactly.'

'That's why a lot of the Ls are upside down and back to front? To show confusion?'

23

'Yes!' Emma said gleefully. 'Well spotted, Kazia! You should be on the assessment team tomorrow!'

'Oh no. Tomorrow I am going to tidy the grave of my grandfather in the Polish War Cemetery.'

'Oh,' Emma said, 'sorry.'

'Do not be sorry. I enjoy it; is why I came to Newark. For me is an honour to do this. But enough about that. On to you now. Tell me about day Girl's Name Emma got her GCSEs.'

'Right,' Emma said and took a deep breath.

GIRL'S NAME: EMMA

Emma stared at the results in her hand, her eyes as round as they could go without actually popping their sockets. These grades were awesome! Miles better than she had expected, especially after the year she'd had. She shook her head in disbelief. This changed everything.

Quickly, she slipped the envelope into her bag and pulled out her mobile, intending to speak to Tom, her boyfriend, who was waiting outside the school gates in the car. As she pressed call, she hesitated. If she spoke to him directly, told him what she intended to do next, he'd try to dissuade her, so, instead, she sent him a text, giving her results (followed by a row of exclamation marks) adding that she'd be there 'in a bit' as she was catching up with friends. Then she switched her mobile off and strode to Miss Allendale's office.

Miss Allendale's smile actually broadened when she saw her visitor was Emma Oji. Broadened and stretched as tight as an elastic band. 'Emma! How are you! Take a seat!' The headmistress indicated the high-backed wooden chair positioned slightly at an angle to her desk then rested her elbows and clasped her hands together as if in prayer.

'I'm sorry to disturb you, Miss Allendale,' Emma began, pulling the chair out so she could sit face-on.

Catherine Allendale studied the sixteen-year-old as she settled herself. Such a pretty girl. Talented artist too; there was always something by Emma on display in the main entrance for open evenings to impress the visitors. What a pity. What a real pity, Miss Allendale thought to herself. Then the elastic band of her mouth stretched to breaking point as Emma's eyes met hers, ready to begin. Best if she got in first, the headmistress decided. 'Now, Emma, I hear you have some good news?'

Emma nodded, allowed herself a modest smile. 'I know! I couldn't believe it! Five A stars and four As! And one of them for physics. That really shocked me. I thought I'd made such a mess of one of the papers I'd be lucky to scrape a C.'

'Oh, I didn't mean your exams—though congratulations there, too, obviously. No, I meant the baby! We hear you had a little girl.'

Emma blinked, a little nonplussed Miss Allendale had come right out with it. 'Yes. On August the first. Tia,' Emma said.

Miss Allendale clucked. 'Tia! What a pretty name. Short and sweet.'

Emma shifted uncomfortably in her chair, wanting to leave Tia out of this. Wanting, actually, to get straight to the point, which she proceeded to do. 'Miss

Allendale, I know it's a late application but I was wondering about sixth form? With my grades being so good . . . '

Miss Allendale blinked a few times then cleared her throat. 'Sixth form? But baby's so young. Surely you'll stay at home with her for a little while at least?'

'Stay at home?' Emma asked, genuinely surprised. 'But I shouldn't have to give up my education just because I've had a baby, should I? How am I going to support her properly if I haven't got any qualifications?'

This time it was Miss Allendale who shifted uncomfortably in her chair. 'Well, naturally I'm all for girls getting the best education they can . . . I wouldn't be doing my job otherwise . . . ' she began then paused, wondering how best to say that if she let Emma stay it would send out all the wrong messages to parents.

'I've got childcare totally covered,' Emma interrupted hastily, in case that was a factor. 'Tom my boyfriend's looking after Tia until he goes to Birmingham University then my grandma's going to come to the house. I don't need crèche facilities or anything . . . '

A spasm passed across Miss Allendale's face, and Emma realized she'd blown it. Crèches and Catholic schools were not a good combo.

It came as no surprise when Miss Allendale told her that the sixth form was full, even though they both knew it was untrue. 'We're so oversubscribed, I'm afraid, Emma.' She said it firmly with no pretence of a smile this time, making it clear there would be no negotiation on this matter.

Emma took a deep breath to prevent the anger that she felt rising inside her bubble to the surface like over-heated hot milk ready to scald. Calm down, Oji, it doesn't matter, she told herself. You've already got a place at Hercules Clay. You don't need to beg. Think about the way she treated you when you told her you were pregnant. Think about how she asked you not to come to lessons once you were showing and how you had to sit your exams in a separate room. Think of that inadequate six hours' home tuition a week you had and how you had to revise in Newark Library on your own. Have some pride! Get up. Say thank you. Do an Elvis and leave the building.

So she did. 'Well, thank you, Miss,' Emma said as she rose to leave, her voice scratchy and uneven from trying to control it.

'You're welcome, Emma,' Miss Allendale replied, grateful there hadn't been a fuss. The girl wasn't a Catholic and could have challenged her stance but it appeared her regime on good manners was paying dividends, even among the fallen.

Tom held open the car door for Emma, a huge grin on his face. 'So who's a clever girl then?' he asked.

'I am,' she said, retaining the same artificial smile for Tom she'd had for Miss Allendale.

'Told you you'd do brilliantly,' he said, kissing her hair, not knowing Miss Allendale's rejection had stripped away any pride she should have felt in her

28

achievement. She couldn't even be bothered texting anyone—her mum Beverley, her dad Steve, Dan, her friends. What was the point? The whole thing was a farce. Meaningless.

As soon as she got home, to a red-faced baby demanding to be fed, her cries as anguished as a vampire's at daybreak, Emma tossed the envelope onto the hall table with the rest of the junk mail where it belonged.

Emma blinked and returned to the present. 'You know what's the weirdest thing, Kazia?'

'No,' Kazia replied, hurrying to keep her features neutral. She did not want to show her surprise that this slim little thing in front of her had a baby. It was not her business. 'What is weirdest thing?'

'That envelope stayed there for nearly three years!'

'No! Really?'

'Really! Until a few months ago. Becky found it when she pulled the hall table out to reach some stickers she'd lost.'

'Goodness.'

'I couldn't believe they were still there; I'd genuinely forgotten all about them. Lucky for me they were though or I wouldn't have come up with the idea for this. I'd been having a major stress trying to decide on a theme. You did not want to be in my house round March time!'

'You were grouchy?'

29

Emma grinned. 'Just a bit! Even the cat threatened to leave home! But then when I read those results again, everything came flooding back. How I'd felt so small that day. So angry! Phil's always telling us to stay in touch with our emotions and I got such a surge of emotion as soon as I touched that envelope! Use it, girl, I thought. Use it!'

'Yes. I understand this,' Kazia nodded.

'So I started playing the "what if" game. You know. What if Miss Allendale had let me stay on in the Sixth Form? What if I hadn't come to Hercules Clay? I realized I wouldn't have met Grace and Leon or James. Then I thought what if Grace hadn't got her grades? She couldn't have come, either, and if James had managed one more C . . . And for Leon, too, even though he didn't take his GCSEs that's had an effect on him, definitely. I read that looked-after kids have real difficulty achieving decent grades, even when they're bright, because their situations are so volatile. That's just wrong, isn't it?'

'Life is hard, nya?'

'You can say that again!' Emma shook her head as if still bemused by it all then smiled apologetically at Kazia. 'Sorry! I'm blathering, aren't I? I'm terrible when I get started. Shall we move on to the next painting? Or don't you have time? You've been a tremendous help already; you don't have to feel obliged to look at everything.'

'Oh! Don't worry. I have nothing urgent to get back for. Only TV and there is no Grey's Anatomy tonight.

Please, continue. Unless you have to be back? For baby?'

Emma shook her head. 'Tia? No, she's fine. Tom's looking after her today. They know I'm going to be late.'

Kazia nodded, still adjusting to the notion of Emma as a mother. So young! 'Let's do number two, then,' Kazia said and stepped across to the second panel where she peered at the title next to it. 'Consequences Part Two: Where They Met.'

'Yep. Have you still got your piece of paper?' Emma asked.

The cleaner pulled the flattened paper from her pocket. 'Yes. It says boy's name Dan and girl's name Meredith.'

'OK. Now you have to write down where they met.'

'Where they met?'

'Sure. It could be anything. In the cinema. On a bus. You can keep it simple or make it silly or as imaginative as you like.'

'OK,' Kazia said and wrote quickly: 'They met in A and E department at big hospital.'

Emma grinned. 'Et voilà! I present to you Consequences Part Two: Where They Met.'

Together, they scrutinized the second panel. It was much darker than the first, applied in heavy acrylic oils of browns and greys streaking in thick lines downwards. Only four specks of yellowy-white, one in each corner, the size of a tennis ball, relieved the grim tones.

'Was it at night time you met?' Kazia asked.

31

'Not night time, no,' Emma smiled, 'it just felt like it for a while.'

'Explain, please.'

'You're sure you've got time?'

'I'm sure.'

'OK; it's about three weeks after we'd all had our GCSE results . . .'

WHERE THEY MET . . .

The September rain and wind lashed down. It was cold and relentless and miserable, preventing any hopes the staff at Hercules Clay had of a bright start to the new academic year. Students trudged in through the main entrance shaking themselves on the freshly cleaned carpet like dogs soaked through after a swim.

Administration staff, their ID cards dangling from green ribbons like Olympic medals, lined up in a neat row behind the reception desk and pointed people in this direction and that direction to enrol. 'Cake Creation for Beginners? That's tomorrow, I'm afraid; we're just doing vocational and academic today. Full time and between sixteen and nineteen years old? You want upstairs in the Woolfit block. Room 17. That's along the corridor, out again through the quad and over to the new glass building opposite. It's the one with the cafeteria on the ground floor and library on the top floor. Just follow the black arrows. Oh, and go carefully with the walls once you get there because the decorators are still in.'

Grace followed the instructions exactly. It was when she came to the café on the ground floor of the new block she became unstuck. The café itself was closed; the corridor either side of it roped off with 'No Entry—Wet Paint' signs. Everything smelt of plaster and fresh paint. Her only option was the stairs and that was fine because that's where a chair with a sign showing a black arrow and '16–19 enrol today' pointed. The only problem was the two decorators in white overalls straddling the stairwell, blocking her access with a paint-splattered plank. One was in his fifties with long grey sideburns that almost met in the middle of his chin, the other much younger with a shaggy haircut and diamanté ear stud. 'Won't be a minute, duck,' the older one said to her, then did a double-take, wrinkling his nose at her Notts County shirt. 'Mind, you can wait all day for me if you support that shower!'

Grace rolled her eyes. 'Ha! Ha!' she told him, trying not to shudder. Her shirt was damp from the rain and she was freezing. She wished now she'd listened to her mother and worn a long-sleeved top beneath it.

'What was it they lost by on Saturday? Was it three–nil or four–nil?'

'Three–one,' Grace muttered. She could do without this.

'Three–one,' the bloke jeered. 'What a shame, eh? They don't get any better for the keeping, do they? Oldest team in the league? No wonder—they're clapped out.'

Grace was about to ask which glory team he supported when a girl came up alongside her. 'Is this the way to Room 17?' she asked, addressing no one in particular. She sounded breathless.

34

'Aye, it is but you'll have to hang fire a tick, princess,' old guy said. 'We're just re-arranging the plank.'

The decorator hoisted the plank towards a makeshift base on the landing above them but continued to block the stairs. He was moving up to the next floor and tubs of paint and rollers dotted several of the sheet-covered steps.

Forced to wait, Grace began to study the girl next to her from the corner of her eye. The girl was one of those types—a Melissa Fitzsimmons type—dead trendy—all hair and bangles and flowing skirts.

Simultaneously the girl turned to look at Grace and their eyes met. She raised her eyebrows in a neat peak and smiled. When she did, deep dimples appeared either side of her cheeks. Grace relaxed and smiled back. OK, then; a Melissa Fitzsimmons type but *nicer*.

Emma stood next to Grace watching the two workers with growing impatience. She wanted to enrol quickly so she could get to the art studio and claim the best workstation. Some of the stations she'd seen on her preliminary look-round had been nothing more than two bits of plywood and chipboard hinged together and were well away from the light. If she did have a choice, her station would be one by the long windows that didn't have previous students' graffiti all over it. She was going to customize it; she'd already brought a stack of photographs and pictures to start. There were some brilliant ones of Tia she had taken with the digital camera her mum and dad had bought her as a 'well done' present for her GCSEs. Oh, come on! she implored the two men silently.

Her stares seemed to unsettle the boy. He clearly wasn't listening to his boss. 'Not that way, Arun, you dipstick! I said left, lad, left!' Emma watched as Arun wheeled left just as a blast of lightning lit up the new building behind them followed by a mighty belt of thunder. It startled them all. Emma jumped but the boy jumped higher, lost his footing and tripped, sending tubs of paint cascading down the steps, one after the other, in a glutinous, creamy flow.

As Emma stepped back she heard a yelp and turned, realizing she'd trodden on somebody's foot. 'Oh, I'm sorry, I'm sorry,' she apologized, 'I didn't see you there.'

The boy behind her just grinned. 'Any time,' he said.

Emma held his gaze for longer than she would have in normal circumstances but he looked so much like Tom! Slightly taller and broader shouldered but with similar dark brown hair, similar complexion—a few spots round the forehead—and exactly the same piercing blue eyes. Even his grin was the same!

'Er . . . do you think it might be an idea to take the lift?' he asked in an accent her grandma would have called 'proper English'. Emma grimaced as the recriminations began behind her.

'Arun! You dozy little . . . '

'Yes,' she agreed, 'I do.'

James led the way back towards the café where the lift was immediately to its right.

'Oh, I never saw that!' Emma said, slapping her forehead to indicate how dumb she was.

'Me neither,' Grace added.

James had. He'd seen the lift and had been about to take it when he'd noticed Emma further along the corridor. He'd stood where he was in the middle of the corridor, just looking, first at her profile framed by all that coppery gold hair, and then at her breasts that curved so perfectly, not too huge but certainly round and . . . God! She was gorgeous! The girls he'd seen in Newark so far had been terrifying. They stomped, arms linked, in hardened little gangs across the market place, chewing gum and screeching. But this girl . . . wow.

He'd walked towards her as if in a trance, coming to a halt just behind her, wanting to speak but not being able to think of a single thing to say. His experience with the opposite sex so far had been pretty limited. He'd had a couple of snogs with Quinny's fourteen-year-old sister when he'd stayed there during the Christmas holidays and lusted over Angelina Jolie but that was about it. When Emma had trodden on his foot and turned round and looked at him like that . . . so . . . so . . . warmly, James had been overcome. All the stuff he'd put up with since being dumped here—the homesickness—or was it schoolsickness?—the nasty little jibes from Imogen—the hunger—she never had any food in—the boredom—all of that evaporated instantly. This was fate! He was *meant* to endure all these hardships just so he could meet this girl.

James blinked, trying to focus. The lift doors were about to close so he shot forward and held them back. 'Would you press the hold button, please?' he asked whoever was already inside.

Leon scowled and pressed the button. He'd been hoping nobody would join him. He hated feeling crowded in and now there were four of them there wasn't much space left at all. Chill man, it's one floor, he reasoned. But he wasn't in a chilling mood. He was in a pissed-off mood.

The electronic tag the security firm had fixed to his leg pissed him off for a start. It wasn't even subtle, just a tacky little box, about the size of a digital watch, rising from beneath his sock like some fungal disease. How was he supposed to have a 'fresh start' when he couldn't even get dressed without feeling like a slave in the cotton fields?

Then there were his new foster carers. Mr and Mrs Cropwell. They pissed him off. What was their angle? What would a boring, middle-aged couple (she was a teaching assistant and he'd taken early redundancy from managing office supplies; you didn't get more boring than that) want with fostering a kid with a criminal record? *'Did you sleep all right, Leon?' 'Just ask if there's anything we can get you, Leon.' 'Don't forget to be back by seven, Leon; it would be a shame for you to violate your curfew.'* Fakes. Didn't they have anything better to do? Like training their dumb mutt Danzinger not to sniff his crotch every time he came in the house for a start.

This pissed him off, too. Having to do this. Stand in this lift in this place. Being forced to go on a course he didn't want to go on. Cabinet Making. What was that about? Cabinet Making? 'Just give it a go,' his new social worker had told him when he'd dropped him off in the pouring rain.

And he hadn't heard from Fazal since he'd seen him in court. That didn't piss him off. That killed. Still, there'd be no need to feel like this soon. Things were in hand. The whole situation was about to be rectified.

'First floor?'

'What?' Leon scowled. The jerk who'd jumped in the lift like he was Wolverine or something looked at him. 'Are you going to the first floor? To enrol?'

'Yeah,' Leon grumbled.

'Could you press the button for the first floor then, please?'

Nobody spoke as the lift began its ascent. Nobody spoke as it ground to a halt with a pathetic whine seconds later. Nobody spoke until the lights went out and they were in darkness. 'Oh, you're joking me!' Emma said.

'Power cut, do you think? We had one last night,' James told her.

'How long did it last?'

James turned and squinted in her general direction. 'Er . . . not that long. About half an hour.' It had actually been much longer but he didn't want to panic her. She might be of a nervous disposition. On the other hand, that might mean she'd need comforting . . . 'Maybe a little longer,' he added.

'Wonderful!' Emma replied but not in a particularly nervous way.

'Well, the good news is I didn't have beans this morning!' James offered by way of keeping things light. Nobody laughed. *Cut the schoolboy humour, you sad dick*, James heard Quinny hiss.

Some lighting returned then, more subdued than before but enough for them to see and the lift began to move, only back downwards again. It came to a halt once more on the ground floor. 'Oh well, looks like we'll have to walk the river of magnolia instead,' James continued. He indicated Emma and Grace should go before him and stood aside but Leon moved across to block the doors.

'Get back!' he barked, pointing to the girls with one hand and fumbling behind him with the other. He then produced the BB gun Fazal had used the night of the fire and began waving it in the air in front of the two girls. It felt awkward and clumsy in his grip.

'What are you doing?' Emma gasped.

It was a question he couldn't answer. He hadn't planned to do this here, exactly, when he'd brought the gun with him that morning; the lift stopping and

40

starting had just seemed like some sort of omen. A sort of 'well, if you're gonna do it, guy, do it now' moment. 'Stand back. Along that wall—away from the buttons.'

Emma's heart pounded and she took an immediate step back and stood next to James, grabbing the sleeve of his jumper. Two seconds ago such a gesture would have sent him into orbit but now all he wanted to do was concentrate. He affected a casual stance, all the time observing and assessing the situation as he'd been trained to do at St Jerome's military corps, though his heart was hammering wildly.

Grace was rather more lax. She didn't move at first, her eyes fixed on the gun that was swishing backwards and forwards in front of her like a manic metronome. 'Now!' Leon ordered.

With an almost casual air, Grace joined the others but she was scrutinizing the gun in a way that made Leon edgy. 'Stop staring,' he told her.

She obliged, instead digging into her backpack and, calm as you like, producing a large paper bag of sweets she'd bought from the pick 'n' mix section of her mum's shop earlier. She had intended to save them for babysitting tonight but, well, she was on edge what with it being the first day and now this. A little sugar would do her good. She unfolded the bag and peered inside. A pineapple chunk should do it.

'What are you doing?' Leon asked, his voice higher than intended, goaded by the girl's blatant indifference to the situation.

41

Grace looked at him coolly. 'Having a tuffee. Want one?'

'No!'

'Suit yourself.' She turned to Emma and James and offered them a sweet. They stared at her in the same dismayed way Leon had. 'It's all right, he won't shoot us.'

'I never said I would!' Leon objected, holding the gun still now and fixing a deep scowl on his face. He wasn't stupid! Flashing this thing at them for a couple of seconds was one thing—death threats were another. He only wanted six months in Briarswood, not more. 'Did I say I'd shoot you? Did I?' Leon's eyes roved wildly from one to the other for reassurance.

Emma let go of James's jumper and folded her arms across her chest and shook her head slowly, her eyes filling with tears. James didn't reply. He was puzzled. The lift doors should have opened. When the lift had descended back to the ground floor, they should have opened, giving him a chance to lunge at the guy and knock the gun out of his hand if needs be. 'How do you know he won't shoot?' he now asked Grace from the corner of his mouth.

'It isn't real, is it? It's just a plastic job from a toy shop or somewhere.'

'How do you know?'

She sighed. 'I live on Somerset Road. Do you think I haven't seen a BB gun before?'

Leon surprised everyone by grinning then. 'Sussed, sister! You win a free trip to Alton Towers.' He tucked the gun down the front of his waistband and reached out to press the button for 'open door' then looked back at them. 'Just do us a favour though; don't tell the cops I said I'd shoot because that's not right. I just waved the thing around, deal?'

James and Emma exchanged confused glances. 'What? You mean that's it?' James asked.

Leon nodded. 'Yeah. That's it. I just need to get arrested. Like I said, when the police come it's cool if you tell them that I . . . ' Leon paused, trying to remember the magistrate's exact words, ' . . . I blatantly waved an imitation firearm . . . but no way did I threaten to shoot, OK?'

Grace sucked hard on her pineapple chunk. 'Nobber,' she said.

Leon pressed the 'open door' button again. Nothing happened. He pressed again, repeatedly. 'Why aren't they opening?' he asked.

'They won't open if there's a power cut,' Grace told him.

'What? What power cut?'

'The power cut that is the only reason we're all still in here,' she answered, with emphasis on the word 'only'.

'Ah! I wondered why the doors didn't open before. But the lift moved,' James pointed out.

'That's because it's modern. The new hydraulic ones will automatically go to the next level down and then stay put,' Grace replied.

'How do you know that?'

Grace shrugged. 'My dad's a maintenance technician at the sugar beet factory. He does the lifts there.'

'Call him then! Ask him to come,' Leon ordered. This was so unfair! He'd done the thing—the act—to get himself arrested. Now he wanted charging and slinging into the next sweatbox heading for Briarswood. Come on!

Grace sent him a look of disdain. 'Phone my dad? Not likely! He's on nights. I'm not getting him out of bed for nothing. Press the alarm sign.'

Leon cursed his stupidity and pressed the small bell-shaped icon below a grille that was obviously for speaking into. Dumb or what? But again nothing happened.

'The power cut must have knocked out the telephone line, too,' James said. 'Nice one!'

'What's nice about it?' Emma snapped.

'Sorry; you're right. It's not nice. Sorry.' He apologized profusely, again and again, distressed at upsetting her, wanting desperately to make things right; to be the hero. 'Sorry,' he muttered for the tenth time. She simply shook her head at him, unimpressed. Think, Glenfield, think! James admonished himself. Pretending he had a clue, he scoured the lift panel, hoping he looked in some way competent. His reward was to spot the emergency number embossed below the alarm bell. He grinned, feeling in his pocket for his mobile but then realized he hadn't brought it because he'd run out of credit. Christ on a moped! Still, it gave him the chance to say something practical and sensible to his future wife. 'Have you got a mobile on you? To phone that number? If you can get a signal that is,' he asked. James was rewarded with a glimmer of a smile.

'I'll try,' Emma said and pulled her phone out of her shoulder bag.

Her hands were shaking and she had to concentrate to stop herself from dropping her phone. 'I've got a signal!' she announced, relief swamping her like a warm blanket. 'Read the number out to me.'

James readily obliged and Emma punched the number in with an unsteady finger.

'It's ringing!' she said, almost in disbelief. She always presumed these things wouldn't work. Better still, a real human being answered instead of an automated robot in Mumbai or somewhere. Emma's voice, like her hands, shook as she spoke. 'Hello? Er . . . there's been a bit of a . . . ' her eyes darted to the BB gun and away again, 'an incident in our lift . . . '

'What sort of incident dear?' the operator asked.

Emma looked at Leon. He nodded towards her as if to say, go on, tell her. Well, sod that. He wasn't going to get any sort of glory out of scaring her half to death! 'Power cut,' she said.

The operator then asked a load of questions and reeled off a list of instructions and took Emma's mobile number. She half whispered it, not wanting Leon to hear it in case he memorized it, then dropped her mobile deep in her bag. Who knew what sort of nut job he was? When she began to repeat what the operator had said, she relayed it to James and Grace, not him. 'OK. The doors can be opened manually by someone in the college who's been trained. The operator will phone the lift company who are going to phone reception and reception will send that person over. See, the system works. All we've got to do is wait a couple of minutes.'

James grinned. 'Excellent. Well done . . . er . . . ?'

'I'd rather not say,' Emma replied, her eyes flicking towards Leon.

Leon felt affronted. What was her problem? He hadn't touched her, had he? 'Hey, I'm not a stalker or anything. You can tell him your name in front of me.'

'James,' James furnished.

'James. You can tell James your name.'

Without warning Emma sprang forward, pushing Leon angrily in the chest with both hands. 'I'll tell people my name when I choose, not you, you wasterman!'

Leon reared back in alarm, banging his head on the doors. 'Hey! Hey! Chill.'

Emma pushed him even harder time and time again. Her anger overwhelmed her, coursing through her like shards of glass falling through space. 'Chill! Chill! Don't tell me to chill, you pathetic moron! Black boy with a gun! How original! Don't you know how much damage that does for the rest of us?'

'What are you talking about?'

But Emma wasn't listening. For a whole five seconds she'd felt proud sharing the lift with Leon. So often she had been the only non-white in a group, Newark not being the most multi-ethnic town there ever was. It wasn't an issue; she'd never had any problems over her skin colour here—ironically she got more hassle for being a 'coconut' when she went with her dad to visit relatives in Lagos—but it was just great to have this experience. This is how it should be, she had thought. Black kids, white kids, mixed-race kids, whatever. All in a lift going to enrol in further education. Cool or what? Then this jerk had blown it all out of the water by pulling a gun. 'How could you!' she continued to rail. 'How could you do that to people? You terrified me!'

Leon stared at her in astonishment, wondering where all this venom had come from. 'Hey, all right, all right. I'm sorry. There's no need to get so uptight. I'm not violent or anything . . .'

'You were waving a gun around!' she shouted at him.

'It wasn't real!'

Before he had time to stop her Emma had wrenched the gun from his trousers and pointed it in his face, pressing the barrel against his cheek so hard the flesh sank inwards. Then she yelled at him. 'I didn't know that! I didn't know it wasn't real. Does this not feel real to you? Well? Doesn't it?'

Leon had to admit it felt pretty real and when he looked into Emma's brown eyes, the fear and anger he saw in them felt pretty real too. 'Look, I'm sorry . . .'

'Sorry doesn't cut it! I thought I'd never see my baby again!'

A hush descended as Emma backed away and sank to the floor, her skirt spreading out over the damp vinyl, the gun loose and swinging in her hand until it dropped with a feeble thud. Her head slumped and she began to sob.

'Anyone want a tuffee now?' Grace asked.

Emma's ring-tone cut through the sound of her crying. It grew louder and louder until she fumbled in her bag, wiped her eyes hastily and took a deep breath before answering. 'Hello?' She leaned her head slightly to one side, her eyebrows furrowing more and more as she listened. 'Well that's just great!' she said and hung up.

She wiped her eyes again roughly with the back of her hand as she delivered her news. 'OK, are you ready? You'll love this. Apparently the man trained to open the doors has had his flight back from his holidays delayed so he won't be on the premises until tomorrow.' She paused, saw Leon's jaw clench and continued, 'Fortunately the lift company are sending an engineer out straight away. He should be here in about an hour.'

Leon couldn't believe what he was hearing. 'An hour? Jesus! You're winding me up, right?'

The look Emma sent him would have petrified anyone less hardened. 'Why would I wind you up? You think I want to be in here with you a second more than I have to be?'

'All right!'

'Why an hour?' James asked. His eyes flicked over Emma's face and body. That baby she mentioned. It wasn't a real one, was it? She'd meant it as a term of endearment for someone, surely? A puppy, maybe?

'They're based in Leicester,' Emma said with a shrug.

'Oh.'

Grace fed a small handful of rainbow drops into her mouth. 'Ha! I bet you're feeling like a proper dickhead now, aren't you?' she said to Leon.

Leon turned his back on them all and began in vain to lever the doors apart, kicking and pummelling them, shouting for help. 'Eh . . . Eh . . . somebody come! Now!'

'Is there any point him doing that? Will anybody hear?' James asked Grace.

'Dunno,' Grace shrugged.

Leon's continued kicking and yelling was beginning to put the other three on edge but at least his antics worked.

'Hello?' came a voice on the other side. 'Is someone stuck in there?'

It was the decorator.

'What do you think?' Leon yelled.

'Oi! Less of the attitude, son; you're not the only one with problems. I'm scraping up Dulux Dusted Moss from brand new laminated flooring out here! My contract's up the swanny and no messing.'

'Let us out!' Leon yelled.

'Hang on a tick; I'll just wipe me hands down. Right. Here we go; press call. No. Nothing's happening. The

49

lift'll be jiggered just like all the lights. We've had a power cut, you know.'

Leon swore under his breath and banged his head against the door. The others stared at him with indifference, hoping it hurt.

'How many of you are there in there?' the decorator asked.

'Four,' Grace shouted over the banging.

There was a pause. 'Is that the little Magpie?'

'Yes.'

'Oh dear! I pity the three of you stuck in there with her then! No wonder you're making such a racket.'

'Get bent!' Grace retorted.

They heard a short laugh. 'I'll go see what I can do,' he said, laughing. 'Back in a mo.'

'Magpie?' James asked, attempting to hold a normal conversation above Leon's banging.

'Notts County supporter,' Grace replied, tugging at her shirt.

'Oh. I thought it was the Newcastle strip you were wearing.'

Grace screwed her eyes up at him. 'Don't you start,' she warned and went to sit next to Emma.

'I'm Grace,' she said to Emma and offered her a sweet. Emma smiled wanly but shook her head. 'Take one,' Grace urged, 'you've had a shock; you need sugar to give you a boost. Go on; one won't make you fat.'

'It's not that,' Emma said, managing a watery smile. 'My mum's a dental nurse. She's conditioned me to see all sweets as evil.' Nevertheless Emma reached in and dug out a few jelly beans. 'Thanks,' she said.

Grace leaned across Emma and yanked at James's trouser leg. 'Yo, James. Want a sweet?'

James, still focused on Leon, reluctantly glanced down. He saw Grace proffering the bag of sweets and also saw her nudging the gun into the corner of the lift behind her. So did Leon.

'Oi! That's mine.'

'Not any more,' she told him.

He let out an irritated sigh and lowered himself to the ground. He sat awkwardly opposite Grace and Emma, his knees raised, his arms cupping his head. 'Listen, I'm sorry again for . . . you know . . . what happened.'

His eyes sought out Emma's for her forgiveness but she had shuttered her face off from him. Usually, he wouldn't have cared whether someone forgave him or not but then, this wasn't a usual situation and he hadn't liked that look she'd given him. He didn't like the feelings it had stirred up inside.

James now lowered himself to the floor, sitting adjacent to them all with Emma and Grace to his left and Leon to his right. He stretched his legs out full length, forcing Leon to hitch his knees higher, took a sweet from Grace's supply, and addressed Leon. 'So, let me get this straight. You did all this bogus macho gun waving business because you *want* us to report you to the police?'

Leon nodded. Beads of perspiration gathered round his hairline. Was it just him or was it becoming hotter in here?

'Why?' James asked.

'Cos he's a nobber,' Grace muttered.

'Why?' James repeated.

Leon shrugged. 'I want to get sent to Briarswood with my mate.'

'Briarswood?'

'Young Offenders Centre.'

James frowned. 'What's that? Like a prison?'

'Yeah.'

'Why would you want to be sent to prison?'

Leon bowed his head and muttered into the depths of his arms. 'I want to be with him, with Fazal. He's the only one who's ever stuck by me, know what I mean?' Leon paused; he was having trouble catching his breath. He glanced up and looked round. 'Any of you know what it's like to be in care? A . . . now what is it they've changed it to this week? A "looked-after" child? Well, I do. I've been in care since I was seven. I've had more foster parents and social workers and key workers and counsellors than I can remember but I've only had one best mate. That's where I want to be: with Fazal, with someone I know, not being sent miles away here to start again. This is worse—this is worse than prison. Another town. Another house. A college course forced onto me.'

'You'd better not be asking for sympathy,' Emma snapped.

Leon attempted to lift his head but it felt so heavy. Blood pounded in his ears. 'I don't want sympathy. I'm just trying to get you to understand the gun thing wasn't personal. I didn't think it through, that's all. I was going to get it out upstairs, when I enrolled.' The sound of his heavy, laboured breathing now filled the small compartment. The others stared as he clasped his hands to the back of his head and rocked back and forth towards his raised knees as if doing sit-ups.

'Are you all right?' James asked.

'He's hyperventilating,' Grace said.

Emma bit her lips. 'It might be another trick.'

'I don't think so. What would he gain by it?' James said.

Leon then let out a low howl that echoed pitifully round the lift. Unexpectedly, Emma reacted to the sound the same way she reacted to Tia when she cried. She looked up, her heart beating fast, unable to fight the innate mothering instinct that was so new and raw in her. When Leon cried out again she shuffled towards him without thinking, indicating with a swift nod of her head for James to shift his legs out of the way. With reluctance and some surprise James hitched up.

Once closer to Leon, Emma touched his shoulder lightly. 'Hey,' she said, her voice soft and low, 'hey. Listen to me. It's OK. What's your name?'

Leon's breathing grew more laboured and snatched as if he'd just finished a long run. His head was now dripping with sweat. 'What's your name?' she asked again.

'Leon,' he managed to grunt.

'I'm Emma,' she said.

They stared at each other for a few intense seconds before Leon's eyes rolled hideously into the back of his head, making Emma gasp. 'Grace, quick, empty your sweets into something. I need the bag.'

'Sure,' Grace said, tipping the contents into her lap where her shirt sank like a miniature hammock under the weight. She handed the bag over to Emma.

'Take this,' Emma told Leon, 'it'll help your breathing. One of my friends has chronic asthma. This helps sometimes if she's not got her inhaler on her.'

She leaned forward, holding her hands over his to steady him, coaxing the bag towards his mouth. Grace and James watched in silence as the red and white design puffed in and out like the gills of a fish.

Leon concentrated on Emma's hands. She was a yellow, he registered for the first time. The recognition both comforted and confused him. Is that why she'd been so angry with him early on? Was that what all the 'you've let us down' business was about? Strange. Colour wasn't such a big deal among his mates. Indians, Pakistanis, Sri Lankans, Somalis, Chinese, Latvians; Fazal's gang had the lot. You just got on with it, didn't you? Found common ground. School. Football. Music. An image of Fazal flittered across his eyes. Trouble!

As he breathed, Leon distracted himself by trying to work out Emma's background. Africa or West Indies?

Jamaican like his? After a while Leon felt able to lift his left hand and place it over Emma's, so she could take the bag away from his face. He looked across at her, feeling woozy and light-headed. 'Thanks,' he said.

'That's OK.'

'What mix are you?'

She studied him, as if trying to gauge where the unexpected question had arisen from, then answered, 'My dad's Nigerian, my mum's British.'

'Nigeria? Where's that?' Grace butted in.

'West Africa.'

'Oh,' Grace replied, none the wiser. She'd dropped geography in Year Nine. 'What about your boyfriend. Is he African too?'

'Welsh,' Emma replied absently.

'Your baby's a Heinz variety then, isn't it?'

Emma shot Grace a quizzical look, wondering if there were any racist undertones behind the comment but Grace was counting something on her fingers. 'That means your baby could play football for England, Wales, or Nigeria when it grows up,' she concluded.

'I guess so,' Emma said then returned her attention to Leon. His breathing seemed to be back to normal but he still looked dazed and could hyperventilate again. The trick was to keep him talking. 'What about you? Where are your parents from?'

Leon averted his gaze. 'I don't talk about that,' he whispered, 'ever.'

'You're weird, you are,' Grace told him.

The four of them sat in silence for a while. They stared at fixed points above each other's heads, lost in thought, roused only when they heard the decorator's voice calling to them from the other side of the door. 'Hello; you lot still in there? It's Kenneth here.'

'Hi, Kenneth,' three of them chodorused. Leon snapped his eyes from the ceiling and waited.

'I've just been to reception,' Kenneth began.

'Yes, Kenneth.'

'What they told me was there's a bloke who's trained to open the doors, manually, like, but he's not back from his holidays yet.'

'No! Really!' James called out. Emma rolled her eyes at him and he grinned back. That was good—she was looking more cheerful. More like she had before Leon Capone had ruined everything.

'Aye,' said Kenneth, 'delayed in Cuba. All right for some.'

'We'll just wait here, then, shall we?' James asked.

'Looks like you'll have to, son,' the decorator replied. 'How's the little Magpie? Have you strangled her yet?'

Grace's reply was a mute gesture using her middle finger that was completely wasted on Kenneth who had disappeared, having been distracted by several fresh Dusty Moss boot marks that appeared to lead towards the just-opened café.

'What time are they enrolling until?' James asked

when it became clear their conversation with the outside world had ended.

'All day, I think,' Emma told him.

'Good thing classes don't actually start until tomorrow.'

Emma sighed. Classes had already begun without her at All Saints. How different her day should have been.

The lift began to vibrate gently. The vibrations grew stronger, sending shudders through their bodies. 'Something's happening,' Grace said. She glanced towards her sweet bag resting, semi-inflated still, on Leon's jeans, decided against using it again and instead tipped what remained of her stash into her backpack. She threw the replica gun on top and snapped the fasteners closed. Me laddo wouldn't be getting his sweaty mitts on that again any time soon.

The four main halogen lights of the lift blared into action then, making them all blink. 'Yey!' Grace said, jumping up and sending sugar crystals cascading to the floor.

The doors of the lift opened and they all shot into the corridor, their faces scrunched as if they'd just emerged from the cinema. Once they'd adjusted to the brightness and the smell of paint again, they stood in a small circle, looking from one to the other, unsure of how to proceed. 'Um . . . you can still call the police. That's cool,' Leon began, 'I'm not going to do a runner.'

James glanced towards Emma and Grace. 'What do you think?'

Grace shrugged. 'If he wants to go to Briarswood, let him. I'm not fussed.'

'Emma?' James said.

Emma swallowed. She looked at Leon for such a long time he had to turn away. 'I think Leon needs new friends. Ones in college instead of prison,' she said.

'I agree,' James replied, 'and I think after we've enrolled we should all go for a coffee to discuss this further.' Leon wasn't the only one who needed new friends.

Kazia shook her head in disbelief. 'Goodness me! Such goings on! And he did good, Leon? No more hold-ups?'

'No. No more hold-ups. We became friends—all four of us. We met every lunchtime in the canteen. We always sat in the far corner where the sofas are. Do you know where I mean?'

'Yes. I have cleaned there. Is difficult to get mop under those settees and those plastic banana plants making for private screen in front of them? Horrible dirty dust catchers.'

Emma laughed, remembering how James had often written disgusting messages on the leaves to see how long the writing remained. 'We liked it there. We felt really put out if anyone joined us; that sounds really cliquey, doesn't it? James was the worst; he always arrived early and spread out his folders and jacket to reserve our spot. He was like one of those manic holidaymakers who get up at the crack of dawn to put towels round the pool deckchairs. Then Grace would arrive with her plate of chips and gravy—always chips and gravy. After her Leon would lumber in and yours truly was usually last and covered in paint or glue.' Emma glanced down at her boilersuit and grinned at herself. 'So no change there then!'

'You still meet and have lunch?' Kazia asked.

Emma looked wistful. 'No. I'm the only one here as a student now. I miss . . . ' Emma began then stopped.

'You miss?'

'I do miss their company, I suppose,' Emma said, glancing away. 'So, that's Consequences Part Two: Where They Met.'

'Yes,' Kazia nodded, her head to one side. 'It all means perfect sense why you chose these colours and materials. And the significance of the four bright spots is clear now. They represent the four of you, so far apart.'

'Spot on with the spot thing!' Emma replied. Once again, she felt her confidence boosted by Kazia's astuteness. Asking the cleaner to help had been a great move. 'Right then,' Emma told her, 'this next one is the big one. Consequences Part Three: He said/She said. I have spent weeks and weeks over this.'

Emma moved the stepladder out of the way so they could stand in front of the third panel. This was hung horizontally rather than vertically like the first two and was covered entirely by a montage of hundreds of photographs and postcards. Juxtaposed with the photographs were speech bubbles and thought bubbles in a range of sizes, such as those found in comic strips, each one filled with writing containing anything from a single word to long tracts of prose. 'I like this straightaway!' Kazia told Emma, touching her arm lightly. 'It is lively. It draws you in.'

Emma beamed back at her. 'I'm really pleased with it too. It turned out how I had it in my mind. Things don't always.'

'It reminds me of Pop Art. Peter Blake and Lichtenstein and Andy Warhol.'

'That's what Phil said!' Emma replied, a look of delight on her face.

'I have just finished book on life of Andy Warhol. Very strange man.'

'Most artists are! I love his cans of soup though!'

Kazia smiled and stepped closer to begin her examination of the panel. As she waited, Emma checked her watch again, conscious of time passing. Her eyes flew open in alarm. 'Kazia, it's twenty to seven! Maybe we should just go to the last part and then you can clean. I feel so guilty that you're taking all this time . . . '

Kazia waved a hand dismissively. 'Pah! Cleaning can wait. Art much more important than emptying bins.' To prove it, she scoured photographs instead of sinks, fascinated by the speech bubbles, her head darting like a chicken from one image to the other. She grew agitated, a little overwhelmed by the compactness and sheer density of it all. No wonder it had taken weeks and weeks. 'Is it important I should understand the words? Because I don't understand the words. I know my English is only little bit good but I would like to understand the words.'

'I was hoping they'll be judging me more on the special effects and techniques I've used in the photographs,' Emma said, her voice a little uncertain. 'The words are just snippits from odd conversations we had . . . though I admit they do tell a kind of story if you know where to look.'

'I like stories. Tell me the story!'

'All of it? It'll take years!'

Kazia decided to focus on one photograph. It was a straightforward portrait shot of a good-looking boy with thick brown hair almost into his eyes. He was leaning against a door, his head to one side, a puzzled look on his face. Light streamed in from the right, giving him a semi-illuminated appearance. The speech bubble over the photograph read . . . 'It will come as no surprise to you to hear that I've dropped GCSE Ukrainian.' Kazia was intrigued. 'OK, Emma, explain this one, please? I would like to know the story.'

Emma took a deep breath. 'OK,' she began . . .

HE SAID . . .

. . . 'It will come as no surprise to you to hear that I've dropped GCSE Ukrainian.'

As usual, there was no response from Leon but Grace looked up at James and sniffed. 'I don't know why you took Ukrainian in the first place. It's not like you were ever going to need it, was it?'

James threw his backpack down on the leather seat and shrugged. He'd taken Ukrainian because he'd run out of other options that would fit into his already cramped timetable, his intention being to take as many GCSEs as he possibly could and gain an A star in every one of them, just to prove to his mother he could. The Ukrainian, however, had been impossible to pick up from scratch and ace in a year so he'd had to admit defeat. He didn't have the energy to explain all that to Grace. She'd only scowl and tell him she 'didn't get it' just as she didn't get why he'd told his mother the GCSE classes had all been full and he was taking hair-dressing instead. Only Emma 'got it'—got him—and she, as usual, was late.

Instead, James leaned across and helped himself to another of Grace's chips, weathering the warning scowl she sent him, and wondered where Emma was. How come the person he most wanted to see was the one who was always last to arrive?

'Why don't you buy your own chips if you love them so much?' Grace asked.

'I'm only trying to save you from yourself, Healey. All that cholesterol on one plate can't be good for you.'

'Whatever,' she replied and speared five chips onto her fork in a pre-emptive strike.

James turned to his own lunch, regarding it with distaste. A pre-packed egg and cress sandwich. It was the cheapest thing on the menu and he knew it would taste of puke but it was all he could afford. Life with his sister was as grim as he had predicted it would be. Relishing the financial power she had over him, Imogen doled out his weekly allowance like some queen distributing welfare among her paupers, giving him barely enough to cover his bus fare into town and back let alone anything else.

James glanced across at Leon. His tray groaned with food, James noticed. Spring rolls, rice, and salad on one plate; apple pie and custard on another. Two—*two* bottles of water. These looked-after kids got looked after all right.

'Hi, Leon. How's the cabinet making going?' he asked.

'All right,' Leon replied and began tucking in.

James sighed. Man, the guy was hard work. Wheedling any kind of conversation out of him was like trying to pull raw meat from a hungry lion's claws. He knew little more about Leon now than since that day in the lift. 'I dropped Ukrainian,' he told him.

Leon twisted off the cap from one of his bottles. 'Yeah, you said.'

'Yeah. So I did.' These lightning exchanges of repartee were too much for James. Glumly, he ripped off the plastic packaging and took out one of the floppy sandwiches, trying to block the smell of boiled egg as it wafted towards his nostrils. He closed his eyes and bit, praying Emma would arrive soon. Emma, the reason he usually left lectures early so he could grab this spot, the best vantage point for seeing her as soon as she walked in. Emma, the reason he stayed at Hercules Clay and put up with Imogen instead of blagging the price of a flight from his dad and going to live with him in LA. Emma, the girl of his dreams.

Emma was blushing hard as she finished the story behind the quotation.

'Oh! You were the girl of his dreams?' Kazia asked.

Emma nodded, staring at the photograph. 'Erm . . . apparently.'

'You knew this all along? He did not try to hide it? Even though he knew about Tom and your baby?'

'Oh, he did try. I didn't have a clue at the beginning. I only found out a lot of these things—about all three of them, not just James—from phoning them

when I was planning my exhibition and gathering stuff. Then when I came to "He said/She said", I had to keep going back to them to fill in answers to questions that kept cropping up.'

'Ah. Good research.'

'Well, it was definitely informative,' Emma mumbled.

'You will get extra points for this tomorrow.'

'You think?'

'Sure! You give two-dimensional photograph third human dimension. Very important.'

Emma grinned broadly. 'You're doing a great job of boosting my ego, Kazia! I should be paying you for all this positive criticism!'

'Oh, no. I enjoy putting learning into practice. I like opportunity!'

The student nodded and, feeling comfortable enough to do so, slid her arm through the cleaner's. 'Well, I guess you've got the idea of He Said/She Said, Kazia,' Emma declared, 'are you ready to write down your own he said, she said or do you just want to skip it and move on to the final panel?'

'Oh no!' Kazia protested. 'I think I like more information about this one. It is such a busy picture—so much going on. Examiners will ask lots of questions, I am sure.'

'Maybe,' Emma hedged, 'but like I said I'm pretty confident I can explain about the special effects I've used . . .'

But Emma felt Kazia strain against her arm as she moved towards the panel again. As she let go, she realized she was wasting her breath. Kazia was too absorbed. It's a compliment really, Emma mused.

Kazia was staring intently at a picture of Grace now. It was an early one of her in her County shirt, taken in the canteen during the first term. Emma had repeated the same image throughout the panel, using the starkness of the black and white stripes of the shirt as a contrast to the other full colour photographs. It worked quite well as a zoning device, she thought.

'This is Grace, yes?' Kazia asked.

'Early Grace, yes.'

'And this bubble goes with it?'

'Indeed.'

'It is what she is thinking, not saying?'

'Correct.'

Kazia squinted at the bubble and read the caption out loud. ' "That woman has so got it in for me?" Which woman?'

'Mrs Fletcher, Grace's Childcare tutor. I couldn't put her name in case she saw the exhibition!'

'And she did not like Grace?'

'That's what Grace always said—every lunchtime just about.'

'Explain?'

'You're sure?' Emma asked, happy to oblige but more conscious than ever that time was galloping away and the cleaner had yet to sweep an inch of floor.

'Of course. Anything to help with project,' Kazia replied primly.

Emma laughed. 'Well, OK. She said . . .'

SHE SAID . . .

. . . 'That woman has so got it in for me,' Grace fumed
inwardly as Mrs Fletcher uncrossed her glossy legs, re-
crossed them the other way then glanced down at her
clipboard. Three times this week she had asked her to
stay behind after lessons. Three! Had she had a 'little
word' with the others about their assignments? No.
Had she made a 'small suggestion' about their appearance? No. Discrimination, that's what it was. Just
because she wasn't a dumb girlie-girl like the others.
Just because she didn't write reams and reams of swotty
essays. Just because . . .

The tutor suddenly looked straight across the circle
towards Grace, as if reading her mind. Her expression
was warm enough but Grace tensed. 'Er . . . Grace.
Your turn to show us what you've chosen for your
Story Sack,' Mrs Fletcher invited her.

'All right,' Grace muttered. Fortunately, she was
proud of her Story Sack. It was the best thing she'd
done all year and she was actually looking forward
to presenting it. With a flourish she reached down
and hoisted the hessian sack onto her knees. 'I
didn't choose a story from a book for mine,' she

explained, 'I made one up. It's called "The Bad Burglar".'

Mrs Fletcher nodded and wrote something down as Grace lifted the neck of her sack higher so everyone would notice the word 'swag' sewn on the front of it. That had been James's idea. She'd never heard the word before but he insisted all genuine burglars had that written on their sacks, even though round her end they used bin liners or sports bags. 'In my story,' she began, 'there's a bad burglar—he doesn't have a name—he's just known in the neighbourhood as the Bad Burglar. The Bad Burglar specializes in sneaking into kids' bedrooms at night and stealing their toys and stuff. He thinks they're an easy target, you see, cos they're only kids. He wears these . . . ' From the sack, Grace pulled out a ski mask she'd bought at a jumble sale and her dad's thick gardening gloves and set them at her feet so everyone could see. 'Then one night, the Bad Burglar makes a big mistake. He breaks into four-year-old Superhero Darius Giannakopoulos's bedroom . . . ' She paused for effect like Chelsi, the previous student, had done, saw everyone seemed at least semi interested, and continued.

' . . . Now Darius can't get to sleep so he's tossing about in his Spiderman pyjamas and because it's a warm night, right, the window is open. He looks up and there's the Bad Burglar, climbing through. In his hand is one of these . . . ' Once more, Grace delved into her sack. From it, she pulled a plastic wrench from

'The Little Mechanic' set she'd bought in Pound Palace on Saturday. Someone nearby sniggered.

'Grace, dear, I'm going to have to stop you there,' Mrs Fletcher interrupted.

Grace looked up at her and blinked. She hadn't interrupted any of the others. 'What?' she asked.

Mrs Fletcher paused to pick a tiny thread from her grey cashmere polo neck jumper, then spoke. 'I have to be honest; I'm worried about the whole tone of your story. I mean, all credit to you for making it up instead of using a traditional tale as requested but do you not think this is all a little dark for a four year old?'

'Why?'

'Masks? Gloves? A wrench? Do you think these things are appropriate? That's what I asked you all to use. Appropriate materials.'

'I didn't put a real wrench in,' Grace protested.

There were a few titters round the room. 'Well, of course you didn't! I'd like to think you had enough sense not to,' Mrs Fletcher said.

It was then Grace realized that her next item—Leon's BB gun she'd kept in her knicker drawer since the lift episode—might be best left inside the sack. 'Yeah, well, that's it. The end,' she said, pulling the strings of her sack together until they were as tight and pursed as her lips.

'Now, Grace, there's no need to get in a mood,' Mrs Fletcher admonished.

'Who's in a mood?' Grace asked, folding her arms across her football shirt and scowling into the middle distance. Stupid woman. Didn't give her a chance, did she? If she'd waited two minutes she could have told her this was based on a true story. Darius really had been burgled, only a few days after she'd got her GCSE results. The poor little kid still couldn't get to sleep without his light on and his parents checking under the bed, in his wardrobe, and through every drawer in his room every single night. Only Grace's story soothed him. In Grace's story, Darius confronts the Bad Burglar with the gun and the Bad Burglar is so scared he either wets his pants or jumps out of the window and dies, depending on Darius's frame of mind that night. Darius saving the day was the best type of story as far as Grace was concerned. Still, who cared? She had more to worry about than Story Sacks. Another appointment at City hospital for a start.

Mrs Fletcher shook her head and sighed. 'OK, who's next? Ellie, tell us about your Story Sack . . . '

'Poor Grace!' Kazia said, staring at the photograph of Grace with sympathy. She had a soft spot for this stubborn girl.

'Yes—poor Grace,' Emma agreed, 'she fumed about that for weeks.'

'And this hospital appointment. It was for something serious?' Kazia asked.

Emma raised her eyebrows. 'Kazia, I can't go into every detail! We'll be here all night.'

'Of course. I am so sorry. I did not mean to keep you.'

Kazia looked so crestfallen Emma felt awful. Here she was asking for her help in the first place and now she was rebuffing the poor woman. 'It's just the hospital bit comes later on. It would be out of sequence if I explained now,' Emma backtracked.

'OK. What is next then?'

'Next? Right. Erm . . . ' Emma cast her eyes back to the panel. Her face softened as she looked at the photograph of Tom, sepia tinted and grainy, holding Tia in his arms. Father and infant, both in profile with the background blanked out, gaze at each other, totally absorbed. It was a bit sentimental and clichéd, she knew, but still one of her favourites. 'This one,' she murmured, 'this one is next.'

Kazia nodded, seeking out the speech bubble that went with it.

HE SAID . . .

. . . 'I suppose I'd better go. I haven't even started packing yet. Mum'll be going spare.'

'Oh, don't go yet. It's early,' Emma whispered. It was the night before Tom set off for university and they were both reluctant to part. Tom bent down and kissed the sleeping Tia on her cheek, then gently stroked her hair. He loved his daughter's hair; it was wild and springy and so much part of her character.

'Isn't she just so perfect?' Tom asked, turning to Emma who was standing with him by the cot in her bedroom.

Emma smiled and nodded in agreement. Yes, Tia was perfect. Except when she woke in the middle of the night and demanded milk that Emma hadn't had time to produce yet, sometimes chomping down on her nipple with gums that bloody well hurt. Apart from that, yes, she agreed wholeheartedly, she was perfect.

'I've put fresh clothes out for her for the rest of the week and her changing mat's been sterilized. You'll give your grandma my list, won't you?' Tom asked.

'Yes. You told me ten times,' Emma replied, 'stop worrying.' She reached up and kissed him. His arms slid round her waist and she could feel the warmth from his body as he pressed against her. 'I hate the thought of going. I can't do it,' he said, his voice cracking.

'I hate it more.'

'What if I just don't go? Get a job instead?'

Emma reared back so she could look at him properly under the subdued nightlight. Going to university had always been part of the plan, for both of them. 'A job? What, like in a crummy call centre or something? Are you serious?'

He met her gaze; his eyes troubled and uncertain. 'Yes, I am. Kind of. Oh, I don't know. I mean, I want to go to Birmingham but I just feel so bad about leaving you. I feel I should be around to help you with Tia. She's going to think I'm one of those slacker dads.'

'No she's not! She'll never think that.'

Tom sighed. It was so heavy and heartfelt, Emma tried to think of something to cheer him up; to cheer them both up. 'Hey, aren't you forgetting something?'

'What's that?'

'The real reason you're going to uni?'

'Which is?'

She leaned in again, jutting her hips into his torso, murmuring in his ear. 'I get to visit you in your new room. Your new single, private, miles-away-from-here room; the one without parents exchanging petrified glances every time we disappear to buy a take-away!'

'Yeah, well . . . I guess you can't blame them.'

'Huh! If only! It's been months!'

73

Tom shrugged and let go of her. 'I'd better be off.'

'I'll walk to the car with you.'

'No, don't.'

Emma was startled by the abrupt tone he used. 'Why not?'

'It'll only make it harder and you need to be here, with Tia, in case she wakes up.'

'But she's fast asleep . . . '

Tom was already at the door. 'I'll phone you tomorrow when I get there,' he called out over his shoulder, then left.

From her bedroom window, Emma watched as Tom's car sped off, tears falling hard and fast down her face like beads from a broken necklace. Briskly, she wiped them away, admonishing herself for being so pathetic. 'He's only going to uni,' she told herself, 'not the trenches.'

'This must have been hard for you both, especially with the baby,' Kazia sympathized.

'That wasn't hard,' Emma stated, her voice cracking.

'No?'

'What was hard was when he finished with me three weeks later.'

Kazia's hand flew to her mouth. 'No!'

'Yes!'

'But why? He seemed so in love with you.'

Emma bit her lip, marvelling at the fact that her heart could still lurch so painfully at the memory, nearly three

74

years later. Tonight, oddly, even more than when she had been collating all the images for the exhibition. She blamed Kazia. There was something about the way she listened and reacted that made the events seem like yesterday. Made it difficult to focus on the exhibition. 'Bet you can't guess which picture comes next!' she asked her.

'Is She Said? You said?'

'Aha.'

Kazia examined the panel in minute detail. If the examiners were half as thorough tomorrow, Emma thought, she'd die of exhaustion afterwards. After a few seconds, Kazia pounced. 'Aha!' she said, finding a picture of Emma close by the one of Tom. 'It has to be this one.'

The photograph showed Emma, looking directly at the camera, smiling radiantly. From the number of balloons and streamers behind her, it looked as if the picture had been taken at a special occasion. Emma's hair was piled high, quite formally, and her bright pink strapless dress revealed bare shoulders. Bare apart from an arm resting across them like a stole. Kazia guessed the arm belonged to Tom but it was difficult to see as the left hand side of the photograph had a white ragged line down it from where it had been ripped in half. 'Tom was there?' Kazia guessed.

'You are getting good at this,' Emma told her and sighed. 'It was his Sixth Form Prom. I was eight month's pregnant so I insisted on only head and shoulder shots!'

Kazia frowned, examining the caption attached to the photograph. Even that gave nothing away. 'At last the moment we have been waiting for,' it read. She knew it was none of her business but she had to ask. 'But he finished with you? So soon after starting university? Why?'

'I'll tell you but it might come under the heading of too much information,' Emma warned.

'I can take it,' Kazia declared stoically.

SHE SAID . . .

. . . 'At last! The moment we have been waiting for!' Emma yelled in delight as she stepped into Tom's room.

Although Tom had been back every weekend to see her and Tia, this was the first time she had been to see him, but after much negotiation over babysitting terms with her mum, she was here. Party time! Bring it on, baby!

As soon as he closed his room door behind them, Emma folded her arms round Tom's neck and pulled him close. Her mouth sought his and she began a long preamble of a kiss; gentle but full of all her pent-up passion for him. Oh, this was bliss! She was so ready for this! Their first weekend together *ever*. On their own. No baby to feed. No parents to appease. No interruptions. But instead of kissing her back, Tom undid her arms, the way someone does on the dance floor when a flirtatious, drunken stranger latches on to them, wanton and unasked for. 'What's the matter?' Emma asked.

'Nothing.'

'Come on, then, Hughes! Get your kit off!'

Tom's eyes darted towards her as she began to undo her blouse, his cheeks burning. 'Emma, we can't.'

She paused mid-button. 'Why not?'

'I'm not . . . I'm not in the mood.'

'What? You've got to be kidding!'

'Look . . . there's a time and a place.'

Emma laughed, thinking he was joking. 'Excuse me; just remind me again where we lost our virginity? Wasn't it in your dad's garden shed?'

Tom bit his lip. That was then; in the halcyon days before the food poisoning that had led to contraceptive pills not working that had led to missed periods and pregnancy tests. To days when her breasts had been for caressing instead of feeding. 'The walls are really thin. People will hear us.'

He began moving things on the desk behind him. An empty coffee mug one way; a hole punch another.

'Let them! I don't care!' she declared rashly.

'No. That's half your trouble, isn't it?' Tom muttered, his tone cold as his eyes skimmed her semi naked top.

Emma stared at him. How could he say that to her? He made her sound so cheap! 'Oh,' she said, a catch in her voice. She gripped the two sides to her blouse together, feeling suddenly exposed and self-conscious.

Tom looked away with a mixture of relief and guilt. He addressed the blue curtains behind her. 'Look, Emma, I didn't mean that to come out the way it sounded. It's just . . . don't you think we should put things on hold for a bit?'

'What do you mean?' she asked, buttoning her blouse with nervous, unsteady fingers. Tom still hadn't replied by the time she had finished. She glanced up at him, saw his focus was somewhere behind her, and grew increasingly disconcerted. 'What do you mean?' she repeated. 'What things?'

He still couldn't look at her. 'I mean the whole sex thing.'

'What "whole sex thing"?'

'All I'm saying is we don't want to make the same mistake twice, do we?' he mumbled.

Emma's mouth dropped open in disbelief. 'What? You think I'm planning to fall pregnant again? Are you nuts?'

She sprang from the bed and strode over to her baggage. 'Look at this! I don't want to go back on the pill while I'm still feeding Tia but I've brought enough condoms with me to last a month and Mum handed me this as she dropped me off at the station . . . ' From the side compartment of her bag she flourished a white paper package emblazoned with the green cross logo of a pharmacist. 'Guess what's in here? The morning-after pill! Subtle, eh? Thanks, Mum. Would have preferred a magazine but, hey, whatever. So don't worry, Tom; you'd have to have commando sperm to get through this lot. There won't be any more mistakes!' She gave the bag a little shake then stuffed it back where it came from.

Tom stared after the bag, feeling queasy.

The truth was, sex was only part of the problem.

Emma's presence here made him feel disconnected. He had been enjoying his two separate worlds. He liked them both; his old world with Emma and Tia and responsibility; the new one with lectures that stretched him and the student life that gave him independence and unrestricted freedom. He liked both worlds but they didn't mix. Seeing Emma on campus only confirmed what he'd been feeling since he came here.

For a start, she looked so young compared to everyone else's girlfriends. Hell, she *was* so young. The two-year age gap between them had never bothered him before but here, where most students, like Cassie across the hall from him, were already in their early twenties, Emma, despite her great figure and her pretty face, looked what she was—sixteen. He couldn't even legally take her down to the bar for a drink! Sixteen, with his baby. It didn't *fit*. It was all so *chavvy*. He despised himself for thinking it but it was the truth. 'Emma, you know I love you . . . ' he began.

She nodded and smiled.

' . . . I will always love you . . . '

'I will always love you, too,' she said.

He wiped his hand across his mouth like a nurse sterilizing skin in preparation for surgery. 'But . . . ' he croaked.

Emma's face seemed to close down then as if it were trying to shield itself from what was to come; her eyes misted over, her forehead creased like the protective

80

metal shutters of a shop window, her sealed lips caved inwards.

Tom took a deep breath. 'This isn't working for me,' he said.

'*This isn't working for me? This is what he said? This isn't working for me?*' *Kazia asked. Her voice was high and indignant.* '*Nya!*'

'*Yes,*' *Emma replied, concentrating on the photograph,* '*this is what he said.*'

'*And this was the end? This was the finish?*'

'*More or less.*'

'*But you loved him still.*'

'*Of course.*' *Emma's eyes glistened.*

Kazia would have liked to know more but felt it would only upset Emma further and that was the last thing she wanted. Oh, how her heart went out to this girl. She had loved this boy. She had loved this boy and he had loved her but not enough. Classic heartbreak. Just like in Grey's Anatomy.

'*OK; I choose another one. Something for cheering us up!*' *Kazia eagerly skimmed the vast array of images and settled on one of a boy with a huge grin, his eyes twinkling as they met the camera full on.* '*This is James again, I think!*' *Kazia announced, pleased with herself.*

Emma glanced at the picture briefly then examined her nails. '*Oh yes, that's James all right.*'

'*Tell me story about James. He said or she said?*'

'Oh, this is definitely a She Said,' Emma confirmed. 'That nasty, spiteful sister of his said plenty to him.'

Kazia recoiled at the bitterness in Emma's voice. Maybe this wasn't going to be as cheerful a choice as she had hoped. Afterwards, she realized she should have read the speech bubble first.

SHE SAID . . .

. . . 'Oh, great! My brother, the little camp crimper, is back.'

James, cold and hungry after a tiresome day at college, eased his heavy backpack from his shoulders and didn't reply. Responding only made things worse but how he regretted choosing hairdressing as his decoy course. The gay taunts were becoming rather tedious.

Imogen returned to pouring freshly boiled water into the Cath Kidston teapot, her many silver bangles clicking against the pot's belly like long fingernails on glass. She was dressed in her tailored black designer trousers and starched white cotton shirt, her thick, shoulder-length blonde hair held back by a tortoise-shell headband. That meant, James knew, that she had a *Calico & White Interiors* client with her; some middle-class, middle-aged woman with more money than sense and a drawing room to tart up.

Imogen set the lid of the teapot in place and studied her brother with unfettered distaste. 'Good day studying dandruff?' she asked, needing some distraction before having to become all sweetness and light in front of Mrs Indecisive upstairs.

'Yes thanks,' James replied, dumping his bag on one of the six rush-bottomed chairs grouped in two sturdy rows against the cherry-wood table.

'Get that thing off there!' Imogen hissed instantly. 'I've just had it restored. How many times do I have to tell you?'

'Sorry.' James immediately placed his bag on the flagstone floor without a word. As she had indeed told him many, many times, running Calico & White from home meant 'home' was not a home but a 'concept'. The rush-bottomed chairs weren't for sitting on, they were for 'ambience'.

His sister fixed him with her flinty grey eyes. 'I've got someone upstairs so don't go barging about with those clodhopping feet of yours. And don't use the bathroom. It hardly makes an impression having the lavatory flushing in the background.'

'Is there anything to eat?'

Imogen looked at him as if he'd asked something obscene. 'Didn't I just say I'd got someone upstairs? That means I'm working, you moron.'

'I know. What I meant was . . . '

'What I meant was,' Imogen repeated, her voice in a childish whine. 'I don't care what you meant, you little shit. Don't you dare *ever* interrupt me with trivialities when I'm doing business.' She took the tray and started for the door, then turned. 'Oh, and by the way, I want the house to myself this weekend; I've got a friend coming and I don't want you around while he's here so you'd better find alternative accommodation.'

James stared at her askance. 'What? Where am I supposed to go?'

'That's your problem, gayboy,' she said and headed upstairs to her client.

'So, do any of you know any good homeless shelters in Newark?' he asked everyone in the college café the next day. 'But it must provide the *Daily Telegraph* for bedding because I'm not sleeping in anything less.'

'There's one on Albert Street,' Grace replied, about to dig into her chips and gravy.

'Thanks.'

She looked at him, alerted by the dejected tone of his voice. 'You're not serious?'

James stirred sugar into his tea and shrugged. 'Actually I am. Imogen wants me out of the house this weekend. Wants to have it away without me around, for some reason. I don't know why; I hardly sold any tickets last time,' he said, trying to make light of the situation but not quite able to hide how hurt, how humiliated he felt for having to ask. He'd called Quinny, thinking he might hitch down to Sussex and doss down there but the Lower Sixth were about to embark on a field trip to Berlin. 'Rub my nose in it, why don't you?' he'd told him.

Grace finished her chip and ran a finger round the rim of her plate. 'She's horrible, your sister.'

'Indeed.' James glanced across at Emma. She met his look with the same glazed, faraway expression she'd had for the past two weeks. He knew the entire conversation had passed her by. Something had happened that weekend she'd gone to Birmingham and whatever it was, it was affecting her badly. She had only been down once or twice to have lunch with them and any attempts at asking what was the matter had been met with a slow shake of the head; body language that said 'don't go there'. 'Good weekend?' he now enquired.

'It was OK,' she muttered, jabbing listlessly at her iceberg lettuce.

A response! This was progress. 'How's Tia?'

'Good.'

He hesitated but couldn't help it. ' . . . Tom?' he asked, letting the name hang in the air for a shade too long.

Emma glanced up at him and he was alarmed at how red and puffy her eyes were. 'I don't know, I haven't seen him. We're having a bit of a break at the moment.'

James didn't know what to say. His heart had leapt at the news but Emma looked so upset and depressed the joy he felt instantly evaporated. 'Well, if you want to have a coffee or something anytime . . . to talk about it . . . ' he began but Grace interrupted. She had been mulling over James's problem and hadn't heard Emma's revelation.

'James,' she called out, tugging on his arm to ensure his full attention.

He turned reluctantly to face her. 'Yes?'

'You could have stayed at mine but we've got my grandma and grandad coming,' she told him.

'Oh, well, never mind.'

''S all right,' she said. 'Pity really. We've never had anyone posh in our house before.'

'Grace, how many more times? I am not "posh".'

'You are. You talk posh and you look posh and you went to a posh school so that means you're posh.'

'Fine, I'm posh,' he sighed.

'There's room where I am,' Leon then announced.

'Sorry?' James asked.

'There's room where I am so long as you're not fussed about kipping on the floor.'

'Won't your foster parents mind?' James stalled. An offer from Leon was both unexpected and not a little daunting. Who knew what the guy had hidden in his sock drawer? In a perfect world . . . his eyes slid back to Emma. Emma, however, was now on her mobile texting someone. Lost cause. James returned to Leon. 'If they don't mind, I'd be really grateful,' he told him, trying to sound enthusiastic.

Leon nodded. It was done.

He reported the good news that he had somewhere to stay to Imogen in her office that evening. 'What do you want? A medal?' she asked, not bothering to turn round to look at him. Instead she held two swatches of material against the light and peered at them.

'I just thought you'd be pleased,' James said before returning to his room wondering how he could possibly be related to such a person.

On Friday morning James caught the bus into Newark weighed down with not only his coursework but enough clothes for the stay at Leon's. James had few expectations of his time there. What would they do all evening? Grunt at the TV screen? Synchronized shrugging? It was not going to be a barrel of laughs, he knew, but hey, beggars couldn't be choosers.

Which all just goes to show, James reflected later, how wrong he could be. He liked Donna and Nick Cropwell from the start; they were easy to talk to and seemed grateful for the chance to hold an actual conversation that didn't end in an awkward silence—Leon being as reticent and withdrawn at the foster home as he was at college. James simply plunged in and made himself at home.

Best of all, the food was fantastic. He had wolfed the lamb stew down almost without drawing breath it had been so long since he'd had anything cooked properly. Nick offered him seconds but he held his hand in the air. 'No thanks, I'm stuffed,' he declared.

'Oh, you'll have some space for pudding, won't you?' Donna asked. 'I've made apple crumble.'

'What, homemade?'

'Yes.'

James pretended to faint. 'Oh, heaven in a Pyrex dish!'

* * *

88

Even having to bed down on a mattress on Leon's bedroom floor wasn't such a hardship. 'Your room is huge,' James observed enviously as he slid into the clean, lavender scented sheets.

'Yeah, it's all right,' Leon called out from the adjoining bathroom.

'You've got an en suite, a TV, the lot.'

'Yeah.'

'Are all foster homes like this?'

'Pretty much, though having my own bathroom's a first.'

'Where do I sign up?'

Leon spat toothpaste into the sink and didn't reply. 'Sorry,' James called, 'didn't mean to be flippant.'

Still Leon didn't reply.

'By flippant I meant . . .'

'I know what flippant means,' Leon stated emerging from the bathroom in boxers, a long T-shirt and socks.

James glanced up at him, saw the bulge round his ankle but said nothing as Leon clambered into bed and folded his arms round the back of his head.

'Sorry. Didn't mean to be patronizing about the flippant thing,' James apologized again.

'Heaven in a Pyrex dish,' Leon replied.

'What?'

'Heaven in a Pyrex dish; that's what you said downstairs.'

'Yes? And?'

James heard the first rumblings coming from Leon and the next second he was doubled up, his arms slapping down repeatedly on his quilt as he laughed out loud, his head shaking back and forth like a loose gate caught in the wind. 'Heaven in a Pyrex dish! You tosser!'

James laughed then, realizing what a tosser indeed he must have sounded. He laughed hard until tears flowed down his face and by the end his stomach ached and he liked Leon a hundred times more at the end of the day than he had at the beginning.

James returned to Bay Tree House late afternoon on Sunday. He burst through the door, upbeat and on a natural high. He'd had a massive lunch—roast chicken, roast potatoes, and far too much cheesecake, an invitation to stay over at the Cropwells' 'any time' and he felt he'd made a friend. Now all he had to do was to persuade Emma to have that coffee with him and life would be perfect.

Imogen was in the living room, draped on the sofa, reading a magazine and listening to Beethoven on the CD player. By her side was a glass of white wine. James was taken by how serene she looked. 'Hi,' he said, 'I'm back.'

Imogen glanced up, raised an eyebrow, returned to her magazine. 'Puff Daddy phoned,' she said.

'Who?'

'Puff Daddy. All the way from LA.'

James tried to stay cool; he mustn't let her goad him so soon. 'You mean Dad?'

'Who else?' She reached out and took a large gulp

from her glass, drained it, and held it out for him to take. 'Fetch me another, there's a sweetie.'

James frowned. Sweetie? Him? Was she drunk? He strode towards her, took the glass and headed for the kitchen. It was not in its usual show-home pristine state. There were used dishes and cups piled everywhere; half empty cafetières snowed beneath the Sunday newspapers and several empty bottles of wine. He found a newly opened bottle of Sauvignon Blanc in the fridge and took that back to her. 'You and your friend look to have had a good time,' he remarked.

'Golden Boy.'

James stared at her, puzzled, thinking for a moment that was her mystery friend's pet name before realizing she was addressing him. 'What?'

'You. His little Golden Boy. He didn't want to speak to me, of course, just wanted to talk to his little Golden Boy.'

She *was* drunk, James realized. Her eyes looked glazed when she tried to deliver one of her deadly glances; her words slurred. He turned to leave, intending to return his father's call, but she reached out and pulled him by the wrist, clasping it firmly in her cold hand. 'Stay,' she commanded, 'remind me what it's like to be his favourite.'

'I'm not his favourite!' James protested.

'He calls you every Sunday.'

'So?'

'He never calls me,' she said bitterly.

'Why would he? You treat him like vermin.'

'I do not!'

'Immy, you sent him a birthday card last year telling him you hoped he died of Aids.'

'It was a Christmas card,' she said, without a hint of remorse, 'and so what? Why should I be nice to him? He was never nice to me. Only you. His little favourite.'

'Whatever.'

'It's true. Within weeks of your mewling arrival he went from "Where's my precious little Immy" to *"In a minute, Immy"*. "Daddy, will you read to me? In a minute, Immy, I'm feeding James". "Daddy, will you help me with my homework? In a minute, Immy, I'm trying to get James to sleep."'

'He sounds very hands-on,' James said defending his father in his absence.

'Huh!' Imogen relinquished her grip, dropping his wrist as if it were a discarded bone. 'Then, when they finally decided to end their sham of a marriage he fought tooth and nail to have custody of ikkle baby Jimbo. Not me, mind. I was nearly twelve, wasn't I? I apparently didn't need a daddy. Just you did, his favourite.'

'Did he? I never knew that.' His father, James senior, never talked to him about that time. *'Leave the past in the past,'* was his motto.

'It didn't work, of course. Courts had more sense in those days; none of this equal rights for gayboys malarkey. Mummy got full custody and quite right too.'

This blatant homophobia was too much for James. However smashed she was she couldn't just come out with tripe like this. 'It's not a crime, you know, to be gay. It's just something you are, like being musical or left-handed. It is just what it is.'

Imogen jumped up then and strode to the bay window, swooping the damask curtains across in jerky, unsteady movements. 'Oh, I beg to differ. It is a crime! It is a crime when you marry someone knowing all the time you are gay. When you pretend you're straight and a perfect husband and a perfect daddy when all the time you're just faking it.'

'OK, well. I guess we'll just have to agree to differ on this one . . . '

He turned to go but she darted across the room and barred the door; her warm, wine-draped breath filled the short space between them. It was one of her favourite strategies, blocking his escape; he'd wondered how long it would take her to repeat it. She'd often done it when he was small: cutting off his exit by standing in front of him and refusing to budge, laughing at him when he tried in vain to seek another route. She was always faster, stronger, one step ahead. James felt the familiar feeling of helplessness and frustration threaten to swamp him. His heart galloped in his chest as he wondered where this particular confrontation was going to lead. Her hands round his throat? A scratch down his cheek? Pinch marks on his arm? Then he realized something. He no longer had to crick his neck to stare up at her as he began to plead for her to let him go. He was taller than Imogen and probably physically stronger. As observations went it wasn't earth-shattering but it was enough to give James the boost he needed.

He squared his shoulders as she gathered her words. 'And do you want to know the biggest crime of all?' she rasped.

He stood his ground, not flinching. 'No. What?'

'Having you!'

'Me?'

'Yes, you! Making a baby in a pathetic attempt to hold the marriage together. You,' Imogen said, jabbing him repeatedly in his chest with her sharp, manicured nail, 'you were the straw that broke the camel's back. You were the reason he left.'

James reached out and grabbed her hand so she couldn't jab any more. 'Immy, I'm sorry if my arrival got in your way but here's the thing. Not my fault. I was two years old.'

Imogen glared at him and attempted to wrestle her hand from James's grasp. The fact that she couldn't at first annoyed her then, as it slowly registered that James was not even trying very hard but she still couldn't free herself, alarmed her. 'Let go of me, James,' she said, a slight tremor in her voice.

James complied immediately and Imogen returned to the sofa, snatching up the magazine and turning the pages so fast he wouldn't have been surprised if they'd ignited. James waited for a second. 'Maybe we could talk about it?' he suggested. 'Mum . . . Dad . . . everything.'

He left when the silence was too loud to bear.

*   *   *

The next morning, everything was back to normal. The kitchen was spotless, Imogen left bugger all out for his bus fare and lunch and, just before he left, yelled at him to take his bag off the rush-bottomed chair. He didn't mind. He just told her to have a nice day. In the end, Imogen was just an angry little girl wanting her daddy to come home and needing someone to blame because he never would. How sad was that?

Kazia shook her head. *'Is upsetting when families do not get along.'*

'Yes, but that's why we have friends, isn't it?' Emma replied.

'And pets. I have cat called Perogi. He is good company; never tells me off for not calling him every night unlike my mother in Wroclaw!'

'Ha! Don't get me started on mothers!' Emma said. *'I like the name Perogi. What does it mean?'*

'It means fat little dumpling! Like cat!'

Emma laughed out loud. Kazia was so funny! Who'd have thought it from looking at her? She had always seemed so severe before, mopping away with a sour expression on her face. It just proved how wrong first impressions were. *'Shall we go to the next panel?'* Emma suggested.

'OK, show me last part of Consequences now,' Kazia began, her eyes flicking one last time over the

cornucopia of photographs and pictures.

As she was about to move across to the final panel, her eye was caught by a large photograph in the centre. Although even Kazia could see the photograph itself wasn't of a particularly high technical standard—it contained every amateurish error possible: the taker's thumb was emblazoned over one corner, all the subjects had 'red eye' as well as the tops of their heads cut off—what it did have was the whole group together. James, Leon, Emma, and Grace. Better still, they all looked so happy. 'Maybe just one last story from this section. Tell me about this one,' Kazia said, confident that because they all looked so happy the story would be happy too. She saw golds and greens and candles on the table round which they appeared to be gathered. The words 'Long time no see' were printed centrally in the speech bubble. 'Was it Christmas time?'

'Yes—well—nearly. The end of term, a week before, to be exact.'

'Oh, Christmas! I love Christmas. Tell me about this one, then I see last one quickly and get on with my cleaning. Definitely.'

'It's a long one, Kazia. Are you sure?' Emma warned.

'Yes, yes, I am sure.'

'I have to start at my house for this one.'

'OK.'

'It's about five weeks after I split up with Tom. He came round to look after Tia.'

'OK.'

Emma took a deep breath. 'Right, well . . . '

HE SAID . . .

'Long time no see!'

'Yes,' Emma agreed, returning Tom's hesitant smile and standing back to allow him in. 'Thanks for coming at such short notice.'

'Not a problem.'

'It was just one of those nights when everything clashed and I ran out of babysitters for once. Dan's at a party but Mum and Dad will be back about nine.'

'No worries; really.'

'I won't be that late. We've had to book an early table because Leon turns into a pumpkin or something if he's out after seven.'

Tom's pensive expression relaxed as Emma beckoned him inside, no hint of animosity in her welcome. Meeting was usually tense for both of them; there were so many things left unsaid, unfinished. Sometimes she snapped at him or was deliberately cold and he'd be the same back. Sometimes—the awful times—she just looked at him with such obvious pain in her eyes it cut through him like a knife. Tonight, though, she seemed like her old self: bubbly, excited. It was good to see.

Tom followed Emma through into the living room. Becky was watching a DVD with Tia propped upright in her bouncy chair next to her. Both were wearing matching reindeer antler headbands. Tom laughed. 'Cute,' he said.

Becky turned and waved. Tia, five months old and sitting up independently now, kicked out her legs in excitement.

'I'd better go get changed,' Emma said.

'OK,' Tom replied. He watched her for a moment, his eyes lingering on her hair as it swayed freely down her back. It had grown longer. It suited her. He felt again a crushing regret at the way things had gone so pear-shaped. Hindsight sucked.

Upstairs, Emma swallowed the lump that always came to her throat when she saw Tom. It had taken all her self-control not to reach out and touch him. *He's your ex, you've no right*, she reminded herself, even if he did look so sweet, so preppy, so . . . cuddly . . . in his buttoned-up cotton shirt and chunky knit jumper. And he'd looked at her, really looked at her, in the way he used to. Perhaps he was having regrets, just as she was, at the way things had turned out. She'd have given anything to turn back the clock. What if he felt the same way? Wouldn't it be great to get back together in time for Tia's first Christmas? Not for the sake of it, though, she told herself. He needed to still like her enough . . . to *want* her enough.

On impulse, Emma discarded the plain black jumper she'd been planning to wear over her new jeans and brought out the scarlet basque she'd bought herself for Christmas instead. She had intended to save it for her girls' night out with her friends from school next week but why not wear it now?

After pulling the laces as tight as she could, she surveyed her pinched-in waist and voluptuous breasts spilling over the top of the bodice like caramel muffins. A smile played on her lips; she couldn't help it. She looked *hot*. If this didn't affect him, nothing would.

With an expert flourish she swept her hair up, revealing her bare shoulders, then she darted into her mother's bedroom to borrow her antique jet necklace and earrings. *Bellissimo,* she said and blew herself a kiss.

The outfit had the desired effect. Tom's face changed colour to match her basque when he saw her. 'Wow . . . you look . . . wow!' he stuttered.

'Thank you,' she said coolly.

'You could be a model,' Becky told her.

She laughed but didn't deny it. She felt like one.

'How are you getting to town?' Tom asked. 'I could give you a lift. If . . . '

'Oh, no worries, I'll catch the bus.'

He followed her to the doorway, entranced. 'Let me help,' he said, holding her jacket as she slid her bare arms into it. He moved up close to her, still touching her long after she'd buttoned her jacket up, pressing himself close.

She turned towards him, her face glowing. 'Well . . . um . . . I might see you later, if you're still here when I get back,' she said. Their eyes locked.

'I can pick you up, if you like. Just text me,' Tom offered.

'OK,' Emma smiled, her heart thumping. Yes! It was going to happen! They were going to get back together! Without thinking, she reached her hand out to undo the top button of his shirt. 'That's better,' she said, raising her eyebrows playfully, 'you don't want to overheat.'

'Emma . . . ' Tom said and reached out to pull her towards him but she jerked back and pushed him away.

'What's wrong?'

'Nothing!' she said, her voice icy, before turning on her heel and slamming the door behind her, leaving only a draught to embrace him.

He frowned, then caught sight of his reflection in the hall mirror and groaned, remembering the fading love-bite Cassie had given him in a club two nights ago. 'It was a joke,' he muttered beneath his breath. 'Just a bloody joke.'

It was the first time they'd met outside college as a foursome and all of them felt a little apprehensive as they arrived outside Pizza Express. James, in a green shirt he'd blagged off Quinny and had promised to post back the next day, was early. Leon, looking flash with an edgy haircut he'd succumbed to earlier in the week, arrived five minutes later closely followed by Grace. Grace had made a bold decision and chosen her away County shirt instead of the home one for the special occasion. Finally came Emma. She looked stunning but felt way overdressed, angry and frustrated all at the same time.

James found it difficult not to stare but still managed to get in a barbed comment, just to start the ball rolling. 'Last as usual, Oji,' he said.

'So shoot me,' she fired back.

'Leon, you heard the lady,' James replied, holding the door open for them all to troop in.

Grace found the whole restaurant thing intimidating. She never came to places like this with her parents; they preferred pub chains for dining out in; places like the Lord Ted where you had a table number and ordered your meal at the bar. Worse, she felt self-conscious now in her outfit. Next to Emma she looked like a right scruff-bag, which was a bit annoying because when she'd asked her at lunchtime what she was wearing Emma had said nothing special, just jeans and a jumper. So what was she giving it dressed like *that*?

She watched in awe as James suavely ordered two bottles of wine—a red and a white. Grace knew he'd got fake ID but the waitress didn't ask for it. He did look eighteen, Grace supposed, and as he talked like a forty-year-old businessman it figured he wouldn't get asked. She would never have got away with it if she'd been ordering and that was a fact.

Leon watched as the wine disappeared, noting how much louder and more uninhibited Emma and James became with each sip, how less terrified Grace looked with each gulp. This was why he stuck to water. Drink changed people; too much made them act stupid. Still, these three hadn't reached the stupid stage so he wasn't too tense. In fact, he was more chilled than he thought he would be. These guys weren't too bad to be out with. They weren't Faz, obviously, but they weren't complete tossers either. Pity he'd have to leg it at half six to be back in time for his curfew call.

They were disappointed too when he said he'd have to go. 'You can't go yet,' James protested when he told them he'd have to split. James then called for the waitress and gave her a disposable camera to take shots of the four of them together.

'I'm rubbish at this,' the girl said. Leon managed a smile.

'Do you have to go?' Emma asked him when they'd finished posing. 'It's so early.'

'Yeah,' Leon replied, 'I do.' He could have risked missing his curfew but it wasn't worth it. The courts could extend his tag period and that's the last thing he wanted.

'Say hi to Donna and Nick for me,' James said.

'They're out,' Leon replied, 'some Quiz Night in Southwell or . . . '

Before he'd finished his sentence the coffees were cancelled, the bill was called for, glasses drained, coats collected. 'Why didn't you say so before?' James asked, slapping him hard on the back.

The beauty of Newark town centre is that nowhere is too far to walk and as the Cropwells lived on Wellington Road, just out of the town centre, they were there within ten minutes.

'Hello again, pooch,' James greeted the dog, easing his shoes off in the Cropwells' living room and patting Danziger with great enthusiasm.

Grace, sitting next to him on the long leather sofa, was bowled over by her surroundings. 'It's really nice, in't it? I didn't think the house would be this big. It doesn't look it from the outside.' Her eyes swept round the high-ceilinged room, taking in the large bay window and rows of books and DVDs in the alcoves.

Leon didn't reply. He was trying to work out how to ignite the gas fire; he never usually came in the living room.

'It's like ours at home. You've got to push it in and twist,' Emma told him, pointing her finger to the dial then collapsing in the armchair next to the fireplace. 'Push it in and twist!' she repeated, looking down to check her breasts were in place and laughing raucously.

'Er . . . is that booze I see before me?' James asked, spying the Christmas stock of bottles on the sideboard.

'Maybe,' Leon scowled.

By ten o'clock James, Emma, and Grace had reached the stage where none of them could have walked in a straight line but were still capable of holding what they would consider to be a sensible conversation. They'd got through the wine and were about to crack open the liquors.

'Hey! Tia Maria! Isn't that your baby's name?' James asked, tapping the label on the bottle.

'Very funny, James,' Emma replied, blowing hair out of her face, her voice slightly slurred. She held her empty glass towards him. 'Your jokes are ten times crapper than Dan's and that's saying something. And . . . ' she paused and frowned, trying to remember what she was going to say, her eyes lighting as she did so, 'and leave my baby out of this! I don't want to talk about babies tonight. It's so boring! I want you all to think of me as one of you all, doing studenty things. Hokay? I'm just a student like you and you and you . . . ' She pointed in the vague direction of James, Grace, and Leon but instead got the clock, the door, and the watercolour of Lincoln Castle.

James, still trying to fill her glass, almost spilt the contents of the bottle on the carpet as Emma continued to wave her glass around. 'Hold still, woman,' he told her.

Emma smiled up at him goofily and patted the chair arm. 'Come and sit next to me, James. I want you to sit next to me. You've got such a sweet, sexy little butt.'

James did not need asking twice. He deposited the Tia Maria on the hearth and sat.

'Let's play something,' Grace suggested, alarmed at the realization that James and Emma might cop off with each other. That would leave her with lemon-faced Leon. No, no, no, no, no, she thought, no, no, no way.

James, his shoulder leaning closer to Emma's, his foot accidentally on purpose rubbing against hers, spoke. 'OK, Healey. Let's be six years old and play a game but if it's anything to do with football you're on that naughty step for an hour.'

'Let's play the truth game,' Grace said, her voice raised as if calling out to someone fifteen miles away.

'What's that?' James shouted back, his hands fastened to his mouth like a megaphone.

'One person asks a question and the other one has to answer the truth.'

'How mind numbingly lame and boring is that?' James scoffed.

'No!' Emma said, abruptly stopping his foot massage and sitting upright, her eyes shining, 'It's a banging idea. I'll go first.' She focused—almost—on Leon. 'Leon, this is what I want to ask you. Why are you fostered? What happened to your mum and dad?'

'Ooh! And Oji's straight in with a deep one! Actually, two deep ones,' James cried with glee.

Leon, who had been counting the empties on the sideboard and working out how much it would cost him to replace the drink everyone had consumed, merged both his favourite mannerisms together by frowning and shrugging at the same time. 'I don't want to talk about stuff like that,' he muttered.

'You have to!' Emma protested, wriggling out of James's grasp and sitting further forward, her arms round her knees, the earnest expression of the neo-inebriated on her face. 'You always look so sad like you've got the weight of the world on your shoulders and I feel so sorry for you and . . . '

'Shut up!' Leon growled.

'What?'

'I'm not playing any stupid mind games.' He strode over to the bottle of Tia Maria, snatched it up and returned it to the other remaining bottles on the sideboard.

'Ooooh, someone's in a mardy,' Emma mocked.

'Fuck off!' Leon replied.

Emma gasped then stuck out her chin and began wagging her finger. 'Don't you tell me to . . . '

Before she could make things worse, James gave her a warning squeeze on her hand then jumped up. He'd had enough all night drinking sessions at school to know how one loose comment could spark a fight; how one throwaway line could ruin everything. 'Whoa! Time out, people, time out!'

Leon muttered under his breath and sank into an armchair. James went to stand in the centre of the carpet, rubbed his hands together, took on the role of genial host. 'OK, folks; the Truth Game. Grace, your turn to ask . . . '

Grace looked blank. She couldn't think of anything.

'But it was your idea,' he reminded her. Behind him came the sound of bottles being clinked angrily together.

'There's nothing I want to know,' she shrugged.

'OK then, a question for you, you little chips and gravy fanatic you.'

'What?' Grace asked suspiciously.

'Um . . . why *do* you always wear football shirts?' It wasn't exactly profound as questions went but it was harmless enough, he decided.

Grace rolled her eyes and was about to reply when Emma joined in. 'Yes, Grace, why do you? You've got a great figure under there; you should show it more. Get 'em out now and again.'

'Get what out?' Grace asked, her eyes narrowing.

'Your boobs! Give 'em an airing, like I have.'

'Why should I? We've not all got massive wobblers like you.'

'Size doesn't matter,' Emma told her earnestly.

'Size doesn't matter? You sure about that?' Grace asked, sending Emma an icy glare. Emma had been getting on her nerves all night. Showing off. Flirting. Then asking Leon something like that! The poor lad! Easy to tell *she'd* never had a minute's worry in her life. Thinking she was special just because she had a baby. Big deal. She wasn't any different from the

107

dozens of girls who popped them out regular on her estate. And then she had the nerve, the flaming nerve, to tell her to get her boobs out. The wine that had flowed through Grace's veins all evening succeeded in stopping up the cautious part of her brain. Right then, she thought, if Emma wants me to get my boobs out, I'll get my boobs out.

She scrambled onto the sofa, her feet dipping into the leather cushions, and whipped off her Notts County shirt. Then, before anyone could stop her, she began on her navy blue sports crop top that came midway down her slim torso. 'Size doesn't matter!' Grace repeated, completing the striptease by tossing the crop top over the side of the sofa where it landed on Danziger's hind legs.

There Grace stood, face set as hard as concrete, hands on her hips, naked from the waist upwards. 'Well?' she demanded. 'What do you think of them apples, Emma? Still think size doesn't matter?'

Emma, James, and even Leon all knew they should look away but none of them could. They stared, transfixed, as people do at the unusual and unexpected. Their eyes flicked several times from the left side of Grace's chest, then at the right side and back again, like children working out a spot-the-difference puzzle in a comic. It wasn't a puzzle hard to fathom as the difference was so obvious. The left side of Grace's chest had a small but perfectly normal breast but the right side was as flat and smooth as any nine-year-old boy's, devoid of even a nipple to relieve the contour.

108

It looked like a long strip of fresh pasta, ready for boiling in saltwater.

As they tried to make sense of what they saw, they simultaneously became aware of the hush that had fallen in the room, punctured only by the low, soporific hiss of gas from the fire and gentle breathing from Danziger.

It took a louder than average canine snore to break the spell. James blinked, went for his safety net and attempted a joke. 'Er . . . I don't know if you've noticed, Healey, but you seem to have a knocker missing,' he said, scooping up her crop top and handing it back to her.

Grace waved the top away. She wasn't done yet. Her little secret was out so she might as well expose it good and proper. ''S right, mush! I am one jug short of a pair. Good, innit?' she grinned, looking down at herself and prodding the right side of her chest like a baker testing to see if his bread had risen, except there was nothing risen here to prod. 'Witch Tit they called me at school. Or freak or spakky lezzer. Nice, eh? The official term is Poland's Syndrome and that, you nosy nobbers, is why I always wear football shirts.'

She gave herself one final prod, jumped down, and got dressed.

'Poland's Syndrome? This is what it is called?' Kazia interrupted then. She frowned, staring at Grace grinning

109

out at her on the photograph. 'I have never heard of it. It must be from Russian side; Belarus. Or aftermath from Chernobyl.'

Emma looked dazed for a moment; she had been reliving that evening so clearly she had goosepimples. 'Er . . . no,' she said, collecting her thoughts. 'No, it's nothing like that. It's named after the doctor who studied the condition. Alfred Poland.'

'Oh,' Kazia said with relief. Poles seemed to be getting blamed for taking all the plumbing jobs in England; she didn't want them to be blamed for creating one-breasted girls also. 'Well, I am glad you had fun,' she said, 'and I am sorry for Grace. This explains hospital appointment you mentioned earlier?'

'Yes.'

'OK. So after this you all went home?'

'Not exactly,' Emma replied, chewing on her bottom lip.

'There is more?'

'It was a long night,' Emma replied, clearing her throat then rolling and unrolling the sleeve of her boilersuit; unnecessarily, Kazia thought.

She sensed Emma didn't really want to explain further. 'Maybe you tell me in one sentence end of evening and that's it.'

'One sentence? OK. I copped off with James.'

'Copped off with?'

'Started going out with him.'

'Ah. I think . . . ' Kazia began. Emma glanced at her apprehensively, as if wondering what on earth she

110

was going to ask next. 'I think I had better start my cleaning now.'

Though she tried to hide it, Emma's face flooded with relief. 'OK. I'll help in a minute. I just need to . . . erm . . . make some adjustment to the angles of one or two of the images.'

Kazia patted her arm. 'Is no problem. You do your work, I'll do mine,' she said and returned to her trolley. Emma nodded, unable to turn away from the photograph just yet, relieved Kazia didn't want to hear the next part. Grateful, instead, that she could relive it in private.

'OK, that's it, I've had enough,' Leon said, striding over to the gas fire and switching it off, 'piss off home, all of you.'

'What?' James protested but Leon motioned with both hands he wanted them out, herding them like a sheepdog as they gathered bags and coats, nudging them bit by bit towards the hallway. 'Merry Christmas! See you in January,' he said, once they were on the other side of the doorstep, then banged the door behind them.

'Your hospitality leaves a lot to be desired, Young Wilford!' James yelled as the three of them stood, dazed, in the chilly December air on Wellington Road.

'What now?' James asked.

Emma jutted out her bottom lip, looking distressed and tearful, then linked her arm through Grace's.

'Grace, I'm sho, sho, shorry,' she said, then hiccuped before adding, 'I didn't mean to be a bitch.'

James grabbed Grace by the other arm, sandwiching her between them. 'Me neither, poppet,' he said.

'Shurrup and walk me home,' Grace replied with a hefty sniff.

'Our pleasure,' James said. 'Lead on, McHealey.'

The trio marched to the top of Wellington Road, turned right then left at Grace's instructions and continued along the road until they reached the lights at a main junction on London Road. 'I'm all right now. You two can go get a room,' she declared.

'No, no, no. We'll walk you all the way in case of muggers and pervs,' Emma insisted.

'Then we'll get a room,' James added.

They crossed over, striding arm in arm along Bowbridge Road with Grace pointing out the shop where her mum worked and the junior school she had attended and the house where Melissa Fitzsimmons the daft tart lived.

'Tell us more about Poland's Syndrome,' Emma said, the fresh air beginning to clear her head.

'Nothing to tell,' Grace replied, sending a shrug that rippled through them like a very short Mexican Wave. 'It just means the muscle doesn't develop in your chest cavity properly; it stays flat on one side or sometimes caves in. You can have shortened and fused fingers and hands, too, but that affects boys with it more than girls.'

'Is it something you're born with?' Emma asked, remembering all the off-putting things she had read while she was pregnant on what could happen as the foetus developed.

'Yeah. It's congenital; something to do with the blood-flow in the womb.'

'You poor mite,' James said.

Grace frowned at him. 'Don't go feeling sorry for me! It's nothing compared to some, is it?'

'Can they do anything?' Emma asked.

Grace remembered what the consultant had said a few weeks ago. 'Yeah. I can have an implant when I've stopped growing. Next year maybe.'

'Are you going to?'

'Dunno. Might do. Haven't thought about it.' What she meant was she didn't want to think about it— needles and cutting and shoving alien things inside her chest—that wasn't Christmassy, was it? 'Eh, bet you can't guess which is our house?' she asked, stopping abruptly and swivelling them round to face the opposite side of the street.

Emma and James burst out laughing. The terraces had given way to semi-detached council houses. Most of them had some sort of festive lighting going on— white icicles dripping from guttering, fibre-optic fir trees filling window sills—but one property took first prize. It was heaving with lights. Where there was a brick, there was a flashing snowflake on top of it, where there was a spare blade of grass, there were streams of coloured lights pulsing round it. On the rooftop alone stood not one team of reindeer pulling Santa in his sleigh but five.

'Great, innit?' Grace said.

'It's brilliant,' James laughed.

'See you then,' she said, slipping away into the electrical storm.

'Then there were two,' James said to Emma.

'Indeed.'

They wheeled back round and headed to town, discussing Grace's revelation and Leon's attitude all the way but not coming to much of a conclusion on either count. 'I've missed my last bus,' James said, checking his watch as they approached the deserted bus station.

'Me too,' Emma realized. 'Don't worry. I'll phone home. One of them will come and get us and take you home.'

'I thought we were getting a room?' James teased as she called up her number on her mobile.

Emma, phone to her ear, pretended to look shocked. ''Scuse me, sunshine, I'm a nice girl. I don't put out on the first date.'

'Damn,' said James, a frisson of excitement bolting through him. First date? Golden, magical words!

Emma's face changed abruptly when whoever was at the other end answered. 'What are you still doing there?' she asked sourly.

'Just having a coffee,' Tom replied cautiously.

'Is my mum there, please? Or Dad?'

'No, sorry; they've gone to bed. Listen, Emma . . .

I think we should talk. Where are you now? I can come and get you.'

'Get lost! I don't want you or your love bites anywhere near me!'

'That's what I want to talk to you about. Are you OK? You sound . . . erm . . . a bit worse for wear.'

'Why are you still even on the phone?'

'Listen, Emma . . . '

'No, you listen, Thomas, tell Mum and Dad I'm not coming home tonight.'

'What? What about Tia?'

'What about Tia? You're there, aren't you? You're her daddy. You have her twenty-four-seven for once.'

'What? But she's fast asleep! I can't take her home with me in the middle of the night.'

'So sleep in my bed. I won't be using it!' Emma said. With a triumphant glint in her eye she hung up, switched her mobile phone off and put it safely away. She turned to James who had been pacing up and down nearby trying to keep warm, trying even harder not to listen. 'OK, Glenfield. Put your money where your mouth is. Let's find a room.'

'A room?'

'A hotel room.'

'Can you do that? Just turn up and ask for a room?'

'I don't know. Let's find out!'

'I haven't got any money,' James confessed, racked with disappointment.

Emma giggled. 'Me neither. Where shall we go then?'

For once, James was stumped for ideas. 'I'll walk you home,' he offered.

She shook her head. 'No. Not going there. I'll walk *you* home.'

'It's six miles.'

'Best get started then.'

They set off, neither of them really knowing how they had ended up trekking together along a country road close to midnight but, given Emma's determination and the lack of options, continuing anyway. ''Tis a starry, starry night,' James opined, staring up at the sky.

'I love it,' Emma sighed as a car came hurling past them. They instinctively drew closer. Emma reached for James's hand and held it fast; an unnecessary gesture as James had no intention of letting go.

Together, singing Christmas carols at the tops of their voices, they half walked, half stumbled along the narrow footpath between road and hedgerow, swinging their arms, completely at ease in each other's company. When they were just outside Langford, a hamlet of farm buildings and a few pebble-dashed houses halfway between Newark and Collingham, James stopped. The thought of what Imogen would say if she saw Emma at the breakfast table next morning made him nervous. He turned to face Emma. 'Listen, loving your company as I am, I think maybe you should phone Tom? Get him to fetch you? It might be better in the long run, what with Tia and Imogen and . . . well, you know.' God, it nearly killed him saying that!

'Why?' she asked simply.

'Then you can sober up in your own bed?'

She pulled an unhappy face. 'You don't want me to sober up in yours, then?'

James groaned. 'Um . . . in normal circumstances I couldn't think of anything I'd rather have happen but . . . '

'Do you know what I think?' she asked, leaning forward to kiss him gently on the cheek.

'What?'

'I think I need a pee.' And she disappeared behind a hedge. 'Don't listen,' Emma commanded.

He belted out 'Jingle Bells' at the top of his voice.

Emma squatted and tried not to mind the cold blast on her bottom. Boys have it so easy, she thought to herself as she struggled to avoid wetting her jeans. She giggled and shook her head at the thought of what a spectacle she must look. The pee seemed to take for ever. Not surprising with all that wine she'd had. Bloody hell! 'Oh what fun it is to ride,' James sang.

She smiled. James. Sweet, funny James. He was right, of course: she should turn right round and go home. She just didn't want to and it had nothing to do with being blathered; the walk had done a good job of clearing her head anyway. No, she'd had five months of being cooped up in the house night after night, weekend after weekend. She wanted to have just one night of freedom. OK, her mum would have a go at her for being reckless and irresponsible but she could handle that. Tom would probably act all hurt and indignant but she couldn't care less about that.

117

Tonight she was having an adventure. She stood up, pulled up her pants and zipped up her jeans and returned to her serenading suitor.

They reached Bay Tree House warm from the walk. James led Emma down the side of the house and unlocked the kitchen door as quietly as possible, his stomach churning. Once inside, he daren't turn on the light. 'We mustn't wake Imogen,' he whispered for the umpteenth time.

'I know,' Emma whispered back, 'I get it.'

'Shoes off.'

'Yes, sir.'

Together they pulled off their shoes and fumbled their way through the kitchen, into the hallway and up the stairs, barely breathing. James pressed his thumb on the latch of his bedroom door as softly as possible. It clicked loudly and he shoved Emma roughly through the doorway in his fear of waking his sister.

He closed the door behind him then turned. His bedroom curtains hadn't been drawn and light from the street filtered through, casting warm filtered shadows on Emma's face as she waited for instructions. His heart thumped against his chest; she looked so beautiful. 'Erm . . . the bed's there,' he said, his voice almost disappearing.

She nodded, undoing the buttons on her jacket. 'Have you anything I can borrow? I can't sleep in this,' she said, beginning to unhook her basque.

James stood rooted to the floor, robbed of the power of speech.

'Maybe your shirt?' she whispered as she cast the garment aside and stood there, semi naked. 'Your shirt,' Emma repeated and moved towards him, undoing his buttons.

James stood there helplessly as she peeled the shirt from his back and wrapped it round herself. He knew one thing. No way would Quinny be getting *that* back.

Emma slid into James's bed. It was cold; the mattress was hard and the pillows smelt not exactly unpleasant but certainly in need of laundering. She shivered as she waited but James was still standing there. 'Come on,' she called out to him, 'I'm freezing.'

He hesitated, then stepped out of his jeans, leaving his boxers on. 'I can always sleep on the floor, if you'd rather,' he said, embarrassed and uncertain and totally, totally out of his depth as he climbed in next to her.

'Shh,' Emma said, holding a finger to his lips.

She had planned on only cuddling James, just falling asleep in his arms, but he came to her and was so aroused and when he wrapped his arms round her and groaned softly into her neck and told her he loved her . . . oh, it was impossible not to respond. And when he kissed her so long and deep and pressed against her, all her willpower melted.

The enforced silence in case they woke Imogen only heightened everything. She tore roughly at his boxer shorts, pushing them down, down, until they were consigned to the foot of the bed somewhere and their bare legs entwined but before anything further could happen James let out a low moan and rolled away. 'Oh God,' he said, 'sorry.'

'It doesn't matter.'

'I'll just . . . I'll be back in a minute,' James said and bolted for the bathroom.

He wasn't gone long but it was long enough for Emma to think twice about what she was doing. It was obvious James was inexperienced; probably still a virgin. She knew she hadn't brought any condoms with her and guessed James wouldn't have any either. When James returned she buried her head in his pillow, pretending to be asleep. She heard him whisper her name, felt a gentle shake on her arm, then a resigned sigh. Finally, he slid his arms round her waist and kissed her hair. 'Goodnight,' he said.

Early the next morning, a sharp rap on his bedroom door startled them both. They sprang back from each other in alarm, their eyes widening as they recalled the night's events while simultaneously dealing with the day's imminent ones. 'James! James!' Imogen called impatiently.

He sat upright and quickly pulled the quilt over Emma's head. Emma threw it straight back down and scowled at him. Fine, she'd be invisible but there was no need to suffocate her! 'Don't come in!' James barked, his voice hoarse and scratchy, not his own.

Imogen tutted loudly. 'Like I'd want to! Listen, I'm going to be out all day. I'm expecting a delivery of stock from Farrow and Ball; make sure you're here to sign for it and put it in my office.'

'OK, no problem.'

'And don't forget to make sure all your mess is cleared up before I get back. There's a stack of stuff in the linen basket and if you think I'm doing your washing you've got another think coming.'

'Right, no problem,' James agreed again readily.

'And don't touch my walnut bread!' she barked.

'Tell her to get stuffed,' Emma muttered.

'OK!' he shouted instead.

He listened, waiting for her feet on the steps, the door to bang, before breathing out with relief. 'She's gone,' he sighed, turning towards Emma.

She propped her head up with one elbow and looked steadily at him. 'James?'

'Yes?'

'I was just wondering.'

'Just wondering?'

A slow smile spread across her face. 'Whether or not there was a chemist's anywhere round here?'

Emma tore her eyes away from Consequences Three: He Said/She Said and heaved a heavy, mournful sigh. 'You were so lovely,' she whispered and walked across to Kazia who was just finishing up in Phil's office.

'Hey.'

'Hey.'

'Need any help?' Emma asked.

'You sure? You're going to be OK for tomorrow?' Kazia asked.

'Tomorrow? Oh, yeah-yeah. What will be will be!' Her thoughts couldn't have been further from the examiners if she'd tried.

Kazia glanced from her mop back towards Consequences Three. 'You could tell me one more picture. While I mop floor nearby. What is the saying? I kill two birds with a stone,' Kazia suggested, nudging the castors on her bucket with her foot back towards the wall.

Emma furrowed her eyebrows. 'Kazia, are you sure? I mean, I don't mind but you've got tons to do.'

Kazia shrugged as if she couldn't care less. 'If anybody asks I am helping student. Nothing wrong with that?'

'Absolutely!' Emma smiled. 'Come on then. Pick another.'

'I think maybe something to do with Leon now. I have not heard from him in a while.'

'Good choice. I'd go for . . . ' her eyes flicked towards the top right-hand edge of the canvas, ' . . . this one,' Emma declared decisively, pointing towards a photograph of Leon wearing a white apron and standing with his hand resting on top of a wooden cabinet.

Kazia stood on tiptoe to peer closer at the photograph, not so much at Leon but at the cabinet. She recognized it immediately. 'That is the one downstairs in workshop. On display.'

'That's right, it is. His tutor kept it as an example of outstanding craftsmanship to show the other students.'

'It is beautiful. What is he said?' she asked, unable to see the speech bubble.

'It's an extract from one of his tutor's appraisals Leon sent me when I asked for things I could use. It says: "Leon is a natural with wood." That was his best kept secret—his skill with wood—or one of them.'

'He had other skills?'

'Other secrets.'

Kazia nodded. She might have known Emma would say that.

HE SAID . . .

'Leon is a natural with wood.'

The comment from Mr Marriott on his appraisal kept popping into Leon's head. The geezer had been bigging him up all last term, telling him he was 'sound' and 'a quick learner' but seeing it written down like that, in black and white, well, it was something, wasn't it? An achievement. The Cropwells had said they were proud of him and so had everyone down at the Youth Offenders office.

A grin broke out on Leon's face as he sketched out the design for his cabinet. It was weird, all this praise stuff, but kind of cool, too.

At lunchtime he mooched across the quad towards the canteen, his stomach rumbling. The smell of wood shavings and sawdust always made him hungry. As he entered the canteen he automatically glanced across to the corner. The other three were there already; Emma and James had their backs to him but Grace looked up and waved. He nodded curtly then focused on the queue. The change in the group's dynamics had thrown him a little. Emma and James being an item didn't hang right somehow. As for Grace, every time he thought of her and her pancake chest he shuddered. It had taken him the whole of Christmas to get that image out of his head. Gross or what?

The queue had moved forward enough for him to catch a glimpse of the menu when he felt his mobile phone vibrating in his pocket. Flicking it open, he was astonished to find a message from Fazal. 'Guess who's back?' it read.

Leon headed straight out of the dining area and across the open quad, looking for somewhere private to reply. He found a space behind the workshops, near some wheelie bins, and hid there while he made his call, his hands shaking with excitement. This was massive. Massive, massive, massive.

Fazal answered straight away and it was like old times. Man, it was great to hear his voice. Great to feel his energy, even in a phone call. 'Just got out yesterday,' Fazal told him, 'on licence for good behaviour. Got a tag like you, curfew an' everything but I don't care. I'm out of that hole and I'm never goin' back.'

'Was it bad?'

'Course. Until I let them know who was the daddy of the pad. Know what I mean?'

'No, I don't, seeing as you never wrote . . . '

Fazal made a dismissive grunting noise. 'Pack it in, Leon; you know I'm no good at all that stuff.'

'You could have written something. I wrote to you every week.'

'What do you want? A medal?'

'No, just . . . '

125

'Great! This is brilliant, this is. You're the first person I call and already you're giving me grief,' Fazal accused him.

'OK! OK! Don't get mad.'

'I'm not getting mad, Leon. I don't do mad any more. I only do cool and calculated. Now listen, guy, can I trust you?'

'You know you can.'

'Right . . . as soon as I get off licence, I'm getting a new gang together. Forget working in my uncle's business like my mum says. Can you see me selling reconditioned tellies and fridges? Joke! I want more, Leon, just like you do. Why shouldn't I? Why shouldn't we? We deserve it, don't we? The crap we've had in our lives?'

'Tell me about it.'

'So this new gang, right, it's not going to be like last time. This one's for the grown-ups. Big time, loads of bling. I met people inside who can show us the way. We'll live the life, Leon. You and me and whoever joins us. Our crib will be the best in town; a mansion. Wall to wall everything. Indoor swimming pool, the works.'

Leon grinned. He could picture his room already. Flat screen TV, massive hi-fi system, some books, a bed covered in deep orange sheets. Maybe a pet snake. 'It sounds fantastic.'

'Course it does. Cos that's what it's gonna be. Fantastic. Are you in?'

'I'm in,' Leon said. No need to think twice there.

126

'Yes! I knew I could count on you, guy. We're brothers, right?'

'Right.'

'Right then. Wicked. I'll be in touch in a few months.'

'A few months?'

'No point rocking the boat while we're both under surveillance, Leon. Head down, nose clean. Zero attention. Yeah?'

'Yeah. OK.'

'OK.'

The line went dead, leaving Leon with a mixture of fear and excitement in his belly. Fazal was back in town. Life had begun again.

There was little room for Leon to sit by the time he had queued up again. Their corner had been requisitioned by what James called The Ladies Who Lunge: middle-aged women on non-vocational courses like IT for Beginners who took over the settees and blatantly listened in on their conversation, sometimes adding stuff like 'My grandson's just the same.'

James and Emma shuffled along so he could sit next to them; James keeping his arm draped across Emma's shoulders as they moved. 'We were just about to send out a search party,' Emma said.

'Don't worry about me.' Leon smiled and took a huge bite out of his Cornish pasty.

'I was just saying I begin my first placement tomorrow,' Grace told him. 'Wish me luck.'

Leon searched his brain. Placement? What placement? He looked up at her and grinned anyway. 'Yeah? That's wicked.'

Grace stared at him for a second then cocked her head to one side. 'Leon?'

'Yeah?'

'Are you all right?'

'I'm fine, girl. Why?'

'You just seem happy.'

It was no use. The news was too much to keep to himself. Leon wiped sauce from the edge of his mouth and beamed. 'I am happy. Fazal's out.'

'Fazal? The guy in the detention centre?' James asked.

'Yup.'

'That's . . . ' James hesitated, glanced at Emma and Grace. 'That's great.'

'Great?' Leon asked, laughing manically. 'It's brilliant.'

Leon didn't bother with the canteen much after that. He was too psyched about Faz to sit still or even to eat. Instead, he stayed in the workshop at lunchtimes, sketching out plans for his cabinet. It was going to be special, his cabinet; a work of art. Something to take pride of place in his new flat. A symbol.

From a distance Peter Marriott ate his cheese and piccalilli sandwich and watched Leon work, admiring the rapt concentration on the lad's face as he measured and cut and planed. Sometimes he'd casually leave a book on Leon's desk covering subjects from woodcarving techniques to furniture restoration. Other times, he'd bring along samples of joints. 'Check that out,' he'd say and walk off again. At the end of the afternoon, Leon would replace the borrowed items on Mr Marriott's desk with a nod and, occasionally, a question. Mr Marriott would answer as briefly and simply as he could, trying not to show his mounting excitement that in Leon he had found that rare thing: a boy with a gift.

He said as much to social services when they asked for an updated appraisal of Leon's progress and attitude. 'I'm very impressed with him. He's a good lad,' he told them.

The Cropwells were equally complimentary. 'Never had a moment's bother with him,' Nick Cropwell reported. Donna agreed.

'He's one of the best we've had. Quiet but always polite and honest. He even replaced all the drinks his friends got through at Christmas when I told him there was no need. How many ordinary teenagers would have done that, let alone ones under supervision?'

On his next visit to the Youth Offenders Team, they gave him the good news—he was on revocation. That meant no tag and no curfew as long as he stayed out of trouble for the rest of his Supervision Order. Leon had strolled back through Newark, his ankle unfettered, feeling ten feet tall. See what happened when your mates came back into your life? Only good things, my friend, only good things!

* * *

It was a Tuesday in early February, about four weeks into the spring term but with spring nowhere near. The cold, murky drizzle that was falling would usually have been enough to dampen Leon's mood but that one call from Faz a month ago had kept him buoyant all this time so when Grace appeared unexpectedly at his side just outside the main entrance to the college, he didn't mind at all. 'Hiya,' she greeted him, pulling her hood tighter round her face.

'Hi.'

'Y'all right?' she asked, blinking away raindrops from her eyelashes.

'Yeah.'

They walked to the corner and waited until there was a gap in the traffic to cross the road. Normally she would have turned right but instead she continued along Beacon Hill Road with Leon. 'Do you mind?' she asked.

'Do I mind what?'

'If I come back with you? I want to talk to you.'

'No. Whatever,' Leon replied.

The Cropwells, he knew, would be out. Donna always had a staff meeting on Tuesdays and Nick had started driving a minibus for Age Concern. Both were cool about him being in the house on his own since he'd had his tag revoked.

As they reached the junction of Wellington Road Leon began to wonder what Grace wanted. 'So . . . er . . . how's it all going?' Leon asked gruffly.

'All right, but the placement at Jack 'n' Jill's nursery's a bit of a let-down . . . '

'Placement?' he asked.

Grace tutted. She knew he never listened. 'Dur! Where I've been spending two days a week for the past month. It's the practical side of my childcare course; the bit I've been waiting for.'

'Oh. But you don't like it?'

'Not much. They treat me like a skivvy. You know: making cups of tea for the staff and all that rubbish instead of letting me work with the kids. I've told Mrs Fletcher I'm not happy about it. I mean, what's making cups of tea got to do with childcare? Course she took their side and told me it's all part of the experience. She hates me, she does; says I need to adjust my attitude. Stuck up cow. She's more like a sergeant in the army than a childcare tutor.'

Grace continued her diatribe on Mrs Fletcher but she could tell Leon wasn't really interested and moved swiftly on to the nitty-gritty. 'What I really wanted to talk to you about was dinnertime.'

'Dinnertime?'

'Yeah. Why have you stopped coming to the canteen?'

'I just want to get my work done.'

'Can't you stay after classes instead? Just on the days I'm there? I don't like it with just three of us; I feel like a right gooseberry. James and Emma don't do it on purpose it's just . . . you know what couples are like—all touchy-feely and secret little looks. It's James more than Emma—it's like he can't let her go for a second or she'll disappear. It does my head in . . . '

131

Leon wasn't listening. His attention was focused on the car parked outside the Cropwells' house. A gleaming bronze Fiesta with souped-up exhaust and blacked out windows. Loud music booming. It stood out. Leon slowed down, sensing trouble.

They'd reached the car. The driver's door opened, blocking his way. Someone got out the other side. 'You Leon?' asked a tall black guy, meaty-looking, wearing shades.

'Yeah,' Leon replied.

'Message from the Snowman.' A fist with heavy silver rings on every knuckle flew straight in his belly. One two. One two. Boxer-style. Leon doubled over, spitting phlegm. The guy then yanked Leon by the hair and slapped him hard across the face twice.

'Stop it! Stop it!' Grace yelled, swinging her bag at the attacker's arms.

The guy grabbed the bag and threw it back in her face like a punchball. 'Keep out of it, sket,' he warned, coldly dismissing her as she fell back and scraped her legs against the wall. His focus was on Leon. 'You listening, Leon?'

Leon nodded once. 'You know Faz, right?'

Another brief nod. It was all he could manage.

'Well, Faz boy made some big mistakes inside. Ran up some bills then forgot to pay. We talked to him about it, if you know what I mean, but he pleaded poverty. Trouble is, the Snowman don't do poverty, so little Faz passed his debts on to you. Nice mate, eh? We'll be back Friday to collect.'

'What? How much?'

The car engine revved in warning. The guy slipped Leon a neatly folded piece of paper as if tipping him, then walked calmly round to the passenger side and disappeared.

Inside the house, Grace cried on and on.

'Pack it in, you're giving me a headache,' Leon snapped.

'What do you expect? I'm in shock!' She blew her nose into a piece of kitchen roll. Danziger stared at her, head to one side, wondering what was wrong. 'You are going to tell the Cropwells aren't you?' Grace asked.

'No.'

'You've got to.'

'I don't.'

'Who's the Snowman? Someone from Nottingham?'

Leon winced as he tried to shrug. 'I don't know.'

She shot him a look of disbelief.

'I don't!' he repeated.

'Do you think they'll come back like they said?'

'I don't know!'

'Is that all you can say? I don't know?'

He edged his fingers along his stomach and chest, slowly, tentatively, like a novice climber scaling his first mountain. It caned like mad every time he breathed.

'I knew that Faz was bad news,' Grace continued, tearing off another strip of kitchen roll, 'I've never liked the sound of him.'

Leon exploded with rage, shouting and screaming at her. 'Don't diss my mates! You know nothing about it, OK? Just keep your slutty nose out.'

For a few seconds she stared at him, stunned. 'Well, that's charming that is! Sorry for caring!'

She stormed out, leaving him with his bruised ribs.

'Tch! Violence! All the time. In the papers. On the news!' Kazia declared heatedly. 'That poor boy. I hope he was not badly hurt?'

'I think he was pretty roughed up,' Emma said.

'And poor Grace. Leon should not have been so insulting to her. She was trying to help him.'

'I know. I don't think he meant it. He just took his shock out on her.'

'They came back? These snowmen?'

'Oh yes.'

Kazia tutted and folded her arms, ready for the next instalment. She had to know how this one ended.

Leon spent the rest of the day in his room, telling the Cropwells he wasn't hungry and wanted an early night. For the next few hours he tried to reach Fazal on his mobile but got nowhere, so he tried his house instead. Nothing, nothing, until about eight o'clock when one of the kids answered. Fazal had two little brothers. 'Who's this?'

'It's Aayan.'

'Yo, Aayan, it's Leon. How you doin', guy?'

'Hiya, Leon,' he began then stopped. 'Are you one of the naughty boys?'

'Me? Come on, Aay, you know I'm not!'

'Mum doesn't like it when naughty boys phone.'

'I'm not naughty. I'm good.'

'Oh.'

'Is your Fazal there?'

'No. He's in the fenders centre.'

Leon sighed. He wasn't going to get very far with this one. 'What about your mum? Is she home?'

'No. She's gone to get us some chips from the van.'

'Oh.'

'I like chips.'

'Yeah, me too. So where's your Faz then?'

'I told you; he's in the fenders!'

Patience, Leon, he's only a nipper. 'He *was* in there but he's not now, is he?'

'He had to go back. He was naughty.'

'What?'

'You can't have chips in the fenders. You can only have chips if you're a good boy.'

'Are you sure he's in the offenders centre?'

'Yes. You have to eat maggots. And mouldy bread. And pooh.'

Leon struggled to sit up straight but kept his tone light, friendly. Little kids would tell you anything if you asked them right. 'Why though? Why is he back inside?'

'He was well bad. He took money from Uncle Raj's till without asking and Mummy hit him and took his mobile off him and he hit her and runned away but the policemen found him hiddied in a 'lotment shed.'

'That is well bad.'

'I know. Uncle's going to smack him after.'

'After what?'

'After he comes out of the fenders. Don't you listen one bit?'

Leon swallowed, needing water. 'No, I guess not. Oh, Aayan.'

'Yeah?'

'Do you know a man called the Snowman?'

'No. Do you know a man called Wee wee?'

The kid started giggling and Leon was about to hang up when he heard muffled voices in the background. 'Who's this? Who's this?' Fazal's mum asked.

'Mrs Mahmood, it's Leon. I was just—'

She shrieked down the phone at him. 'No! Don't phone here again, Leon, or I'll call the police like I told the others. This is harassment. Keep away. Keep away.'

Leon stared into the phone. What the hell was going on?

He didn't go to college the next day either. He feigned illness; a cough to cover up the pain when his ribs hurt. At least one was broken, he was sure of it.

From his bedroom window, he watched the street, waiting for the car, wondering if it would return early. Nothing so far. In between, he tried Fazal's mobile number, pressing 'call' repeatedly. Nada. He tried Mrs

Mahmood again, too, but as soon as she knew it was Leon, she hung up. Mostly she had the phone off the hook.

The whole thing had totally fazed him. If this was some sort of wind-up . . . an initiation ceremony to test him out? Fazal had said the new gang wouldn't be like last time, little kids playing at it but . . . come on! There was taking things serious and being psycho. What then? This thing was for real? If so, he was a dead man. No way did he have anything like the amount on the note. All those noughts? You had to be kidding.

Against all his principles he had been to the bank and withdrawn a chunk of his savings—the curfew meant he didn't spend the allowance he had from social services or the money for attending college, so he had cash—but he hated the thought of just handing it over.

One thing was for sure, Fazal had some explaining to do, but if he couldn't get hold of him before next week, what then? In the end, he did the only thing he could think of doing; he wrote to him, hoping he'd be at the same detention centre as before, if he was in one at all. He didn't buy the story of Fazal being banged up again. Why would Fazal do that? He'd been so happy to get out, full of plans. That Aayan was a canny little liar in on the whole game for all he knew.

He kept the letter short and to the point. Drew a snowman with an arrow and a question mark. You'd better write back this time, Faz, he thought, you'd better write back.

* * *

Grace had the hump with Leon for two days. How dare he talk to her like that? Who did he think he was? He could rot in hell for all she cared. She hoped the Snowman beat seven bells out of him. Even so on Friday morning she woke feeling anxious. They were coming back today, weren't they? What if they killed him and she did nothing to stop them? How could she live with herself? Leon might be mardy and rude sometimes— not to mention the incident in the lift—but deep down there was no real harm in him. It was no good; she'd have to do something. From the bottom of her knicker drawer she pulled out the BB gun and wrapped it in her County scarf.

On her way to lectures she called in at the cabinet making workshop and asked one of the lads if they had seen Leon. 'Hasn't been in for days,' he told her. That didn't help ease her growing discomfort one iota.

At lunchtime she waited for a gap in the conversation to tell Emma and James about Leon but Emma was in the middle of her own little crisis and that was taking priority. Her grandma had shingles and the doctor had told her it's because she's doing too much so she'd told Emma once she was better she couldn't look after Tia any more. 'I've spent all morning trying to find a place for her in a nursery but everyone's full. I don't know what I'm supposed to do. Mum's taken two days off work already but she can't use up any more of her holidays. Nightmare. Complete nightmare.'

'I thought there was a crèche here?' James said trying to be helpful.

'They don't take under twos,' Emma grumbled, scrolling down for Tom's number, scowling as she reached Tom's answering service *again*. Angrily, she left another curt message.

'I need to talk to you both,' Grace said.

Emma looked at her, unseeing for a moment then her eyes opened wide in hope. 'Grace! Your tutors would know, wouldn't they? They might have a list of recommended childminders or something.'

'I don't know. I could ask,' Grace replied.

'Sorted.' Emma beamed then took a final sip of her coffee and announced she had to get to the studio to catch up with her painting assignment while she had the chance.

Thinking it might be better to leave Emma out of things anyway, Grace turned to James. 'James,' Grace began, 'I need to tell you something about Leon.'

James, his eyes following Emma out of the cafeteria, was already gathering his folders together, preparing to leave. He didn't even glance up at her as he replied. 'Yeah, later, Grace,' he told her and darted away. Charming.

They were coming. He knew it. Could feel it every time he breathed in. Fear made him indecisive, clogged up his brain like an arsonist's rags in a letterbox. Run. That's what his instincts had been. Run. But the shame

139

of it all was he had nowhere to run to. Kids in care never did.

He moved across from his bedroom window and checked the money in the envelope for the hundredth time. What time was it? Three o'clock. He had an hour, maybe.

Taking the envelope, he made his way down the stairs. The house felt empty and oppressive, like a funeral parlour full of empty caskets. Donna, he knew, wouldn't be home until almost six and Nick maybe a bit earlier than that but not much. He was alone.

He couldn't face sitting in the bright, cheery kitchen. Instead, he headed for the front door and lowered himself bit by bit so as not to hurt his ribs, so that his back leaned against one wall and he faced the other. For a passing moment it reminded him of being in the lift and he felt panic rise in him but he shrugged it off. The ceiling was higher. There was a draught from the gaps in the door; he was surrounded by space. Best of all, he could walk away whenever he wanted. This was nothing like being stuck in a lift with James and the others. And it was definitely not like that time when he was seven. It was nothing like that.

Leon shuddered, squeezed his eyes shut at the memory. Blocking it out like he always did again and again and again. His breathing quickened and he began to sweat. *Stay cool*, he commanded himself, tracing his finger round the cold mosaic tiles. It eased him. Did the trick. He had other things to obsess about now.

From time to time he slipped his hands into his pockets, checking the envelope was in the left one, the knife in the right. The knife, taken from Donna's cutlery drawer. Long and sharp for chopping meat. If these chancers wanted a fight they could have one. Carefully he withdrew it from his pocket and left it by his side, ready.

By the time Mrs Fletcher began dismissing them and telling them all to have a nice weekend, Grace was already out of the classroom and flying towards the main entrance.

She got as far as the sandstone columns outside when she stopped dead, her heart pounding as loudly as the music coming from the car that was driving so, so slowly past the college. The anonymous driver behind the blacked-out windows seemed unperturbed by the queue of traffic behind it, taking his time as if leading a rapper's funeral cortège. Grace darted behind the robust column, using its girth like a bouncer in a nightclub, feeling protected, at least for a short while.

The car then disappeared from sight, heading for Leon.

He heard the music first. The muted boom-boom-boom coming from the car. Then a menacing silence as it was switched off. Almost immediately there was a knock on the door. Leon unfurled himself and stood upright, keeping his back against the wall. At the same time, Danziger padded in from the kitchen, barking at the noise. Somehow, even though barking was all she was good for, it helped.

'Who is it?' he asked, trying to sound sharp, in control.

'You know who it is, Leon.'

The voice caught him out. It was a girl's and she had a slight lisp.

'What do you want?'

'You know what we want. Don't mess about, please. I've left my friend in the car—the one you met last week—and he doesn't like to be cooped up too long.'

'I'm not coming out. If you want the money, put your hand through the letterbox for it.'

'With Danziger there? I don't think so.'

Leon frowned. How did they know the dog's name?

Danziger was now lying on the floor, licking her belly. She'd be as much use as a chocolate teapot in a fight. Did they know that, too? 'It's that or nothing.'

There was a pause. 'OK, but I hope you're not going to try anything, Leon, it wouldn't be in your interests, or Danziger's, or Grace's or James's or Emma's.'

Sweat prickled under his armpits. What? They knew them, too? He withdrew the crumpled envelope and stared at it. 'Ready?' he said.

'Ready.'

The letterbox creaked open. A small white hand with slim, bloodless fingers slid through like a tapeworm searching for a fresh host to suck. Leon felt repulsed and thrust the envelope at the hand, turning away until he heard the flap thwack back into place.

He waited, feeling slightly sick, knowing she was still there, counting it. 'It's not enough,' she said. Her voice sounded more sad and disappointed than angry.

'It's all I've got.' Leon felt for the knife in his pocket; realized it was still on the floor. He bent quickly to retrieve it, flinching as his ribs blazed in his chest. Danziger stopped licking and wagged her tail in sympathy.

'Oh, Leon, that means we have to come back. I'm going to have to add petrol money now, too.'

Was that a joke? 'It's all I've got,' he repeated.

'You know what, I believe you. The trouble is we still want the rest.'

'Where am I supposed to get it?'

'I don't know. I'm really sorry; it must be a real worry for you.'

Leon frowned. Was she for real? 'By the way, Leon?' she continued.

'What?'

'You really don't need to skive off college throughout all this. We were killing time earlier and didn't see you there at all. Education is vital, you know.'

He couldn't believe what he was hearing. She sounded more like one of his social workers than a blackmailer. 'What?' he asked again in disbelief.

'Just saying! Don't follow Fazal's example, that's all. It's him being as thick as pig shit that got you into this mess in the first place.'

'Thanks for the tip.'

'Yeah, well. Only trying to help. We feel sorry for you. We know you've had a hard life, Leon. That thing with your mum and dad was awful.'

'What? Who told you about them? Who told you?' Leon asked urgently.

'Who do you think?'

'He wouldn't. Faz knows we don't talk about that stuff. He knows.'

'You talk about anything when you're banged up twenty hours a day, Leon. Don't worry. It won't go any further. It's too sad, though. Too sad what happened.'

No! They couldn't know. Not these scumbags. Leon screamed at the door, making Danziger bark loudly. 'Shut your face! Shut it!' he yelled at the unseen figure on the other side.

The girl's remorseful tone sharpened instantly. 'Don't be like that, Leon. That's not a nice thing to say to someone at all. We're giving you a second chance. We don't usually give people a second chance.'

'I'm *so* grateful,' Leon snarled, one hand curling round the knife, the other moving towards the door handle. Danziger stopped barking and wagged her tail instead, thinking walkies were on the agenda.

There was a pause before the girl replied. This time her voice was as cold as the knife blade in his palm. 'We're going now, Leon. You can have your little paddy in peace, then. But just so as you know: next time, if the money's not all there, you won't be let off so lightly. And that's a promise *and* a threat.' Then she added incongruously, 'See ya, wouldn't want to be ya!'

He heard footsteps retreat and the car drive off but it was only when Danziger started nuzzling him, whining as if sensing Leon's anguish, that he moved away from the door and returned to the kitchen.

'All you have to do is walk by the house. How hard is that!' Grace was saying to James.

He looked at her and shook his head, continuing across the quad. He wasn't getting involved in gang warfare. Ridiculous. 'No!' he barked.

Grace measured him stride for stride, becoming angrier and angrier. 'Leon needs our help!'

'I told you. Call the police. There's a state of the art police station within spitting distance.'

'Oh, where've you been all your life! Get a clue.'

'Sorry. I thought that's what they were there for.'

Grace stopped, adjusted her shoulder bag, and pulled at the strap of her crop top. 'So you're not coming? Fine, I'll go on my own.'

James let out an exaggerated sigh. Bloody hell. Nothing like this happened at St Jerome's. 'Wait,' he said and grabbed Grace's arm. It felt surprisingly solid. 'All right. I'll come.'

'Should think so,' she replied, leading the way in the opposite direction, pushing through the stragglers and wasters who had time to stroll and chat. 'Maybe we should bring Emma, too,' Grace said over her shoulder.

'Yeah, that would be better. Get her to bring all her friends from her art course, especially any lads.'

James shook his head emphatically. 'No! I'm not involving Emma. It's all too . . . '

'Too what?' Grace asked, blowing her wispy hair out of her face.

'Too weird.' Too common, he meant. Too . . . sleazy.

'There she is,' Grace said, pointing to Emma who was about to get into a car parked by the roadside.

'Leave it,' James demanded, frowning as he realized the almost new Mini Cooper with go-fast red stripes across the roof and bonnet must be Tom's car. What was he doing here? James's stomach clenched with the onset of the jealousy he somehow couldn't combat where Tom was concerned. Well, it was a big ask not to be jealous, he reckoned, accepting that his girlfriend's ex was always going to be in the background.

'Come on!' Grace beckoned. 'A car's useful for if we need a quick getaway.'

'Of course it is, Miss Moneypenny,' James muttered.

At the kerbside, James stood apart from the scene, leaning against the railings, his hands in his pockets, trying to look nonchalant as Grace launched into the incredible story. Emma's face changed from frown to consternation to disbelief. She glanced across at him for confirmation and he shrugged and tried to smile. 'We'd better go there this minute then!' Emma cried and flung open the passenger door to garble orders at Tom. 'Come on,' she ordered James and Grace, ushering them into the back of the Mini.

James was relieved the journey was a short one. Staring at the back of Tom's head for longer would have been too much.

It was Grace who was the first to see the bronze car tearing down Wellington Road. 'That's it, that's it!' she screamed.

'Bloody hell!' James exclaimed as the whole scenario became real and therefore more surreal.

Tom pulled up, unhurried and neatly, as if taking his driving test, outside the Cropwells' house. All four paused for a second to look for signs; broken glass, pools of blood, limbs, but apart from an empty crisp packet caught in the bars of the gate there was nothing.

Tom emerged first, pulling his seat forward so Grace and James could get out too. Emma opened the door on her side, intending to follow but Tom shook his head. 'What?' she asked, watching Grace dash up the path with James.

'We've got to get back for Tia.'

'We can spare five minutes! This is a bit more urgent, isn't it?'

Tom glanced towards the house. 'I'm not sure I want you mixed up in all this.'

'Tough,' she said and began to walk away. James waited, reaching a hand out for her to hold, feeling reassured as if Emma had chosen him over Tom.

Then Tom called out, 'Hang on,' before joining them, a hefty metal steering wheel lock in his hand.

'Good thinking,' Emma told him.

'Damn,' James muttered beneath his breath, wishing he'd thought of it.

The four of them waited for what seemed like hours until Leon opened the door. He looked dazed when he saw them, letting them in without a word. They all walked through into the kitchen. 'Look,' he said, his eyes roaming from one to the other like an overwhelmed actor facing the cameras, 'thanks for coming and everything but the Cropwells'll be back soon and I need some space.'

'I'm going nowhere,' Grace declared, pulling out a chair and plonking herself down on it.

'And I've missed my bus so if there's a coffee going . . . ' James added.

Emma stood up, thinking at least one person should listen to the poor guy. 'We'll go, Leon,' she said, 'as long as you're OK. We've got to get back for Tia anyway.'

She avoided looking directly at James, anticipating his lost, hard-done-by expression. She would call him later but Tia's childcare needed sorting; she had two more childminders to check out with Tom this evening and if he didn't *get* that . . .

As she followed Tom towards the door, Leon called out to her. 'Wait!' he said, edging his way round the table, past Emma to stand in front of Tom. 'Have you got a car?' he asked him.

Tom glanced down at the redundant wheel lock. 'Er . . . yes.'

'And you're over eighteen, right?'

'Yes again.'

A look, half pain, half relief, crossed Leon's face. 'Can I have a word?' he said, leading Tom into the hallway.

'What was that about?' Emma asked Tom as they returned to the car.

'I'm taking Leon to Briarswood tomorrow.'

'What? The detention centre? Why?'

'That's where his friend is. He reckons if he sees him he'll get to the root of all this. Apparently this Fazal sent him a visitor's order this morning but you have to be eighteen or with someone who's eighteen to use it.'

Emma stared at Tom in amazement. 'I thought you didn't want to get mixed up in all this?' she said.

Tom shrugged, threw the wheel lock onto the back seat and glanced at her.

'Leon's a friend of yours, isn't he?'

'Yes.'

'Then that's all that counts.'

'Oh,' was all James said to Emma that night when she told him what was happening.

The waiting room was grim. Bare, pale grey walls and full of utility furniture mingled with an air of desperation and aborted sentences. Dispassionate surveillance cameras and bored but alert officers watched every move.

'So, tell me about the Snowman,' Leon said, leaning his elbows as far forward on the grey formica table as he knew he was allowed. The rules had been made very clear at reception while he was being searched. Limited physical contact only.

Fazal seemed affronted by the abrupt greeting. 'Nice to see you too, bud. Haven't you brought me anything?'

'What like?' Leon asked coldly. It still hurt him that Fazal had told the blackmailers about his mum and dad. Faz, of all people, the one person in the world he thought he could trust.

'A Mars bar. Snickers. Anything,' Fazal elaborated.

Leon shook his head. 'No.' It hadn't occurred to him to bring anything. He'd forgotten what a sweet tooth his friend had.

Fazal pouted, turned to Tom. 'What about you? You got any chocolate on you, mate?'

Tom looked up from the book he was reading. 'No, sorry.'

'Fuh!'

'Faz,' Leon said, trying to keep him on track, 'tell me about the Snowman.'

Fazal sighed, scratched his navy blue regulation sweatshirt from which his thin neck protruded like a tulip stalk. 'He was a lad I shared my pad with. Weird little monkey but better than the one I had before. Savage. He was savage and all. Nicked all my stuff. Had my phone cards away. Real nice chappie.'

Leon frowned. It seemed incredible to him that Fazal would let anyone get away with that. Yet looking at him properly he could see he had changed. His face was more hollowed out, framed by a short and severe haircut that emphasized his round brown eyes, making him look more marsupial than man. Fazal seemed altogether smaller, somehow, a mini-me version of himself. The strut and swagger he'd last seen in the magistrate's court had been knocked out of him. It shocked Leon, disappointed him even, making him harsher than he intended. 'Never mind Savage. What about the Snowman?'

'I'm getting to that if you'll listen,' Fazal responded angrily. First no chocolate and now the attitude from his so-called best mate. 'Savage left me his double bubble, that's how the mess started in the first place.'

'Double bubble?'

Faz glanced across at the next table where another inmate he didn't recognize was being given a mouthful by his missus. Nevertheless Faz lowered his voice so it was almost a whisper. 'If you owe money in here and get out before you've paid it back, whoever gets your bed gets your debt. With interest. That's double bubble. Savage made me swap his top bunk with my bottom one before he left. I thought he was being sporting, like, letting me have the best view of the telly and that but was he 'eck. Set me up good and proper, didn't he? Inherited all his debt and I mean all of it; he'd been inside for two years! Course, I couldn't pay, could I? You know money doesn't exactly grow on trees in our house, does it? If I got a fiver a week from my mum I was laughing. Anyway, I was getting a lot of grief about it from the others till Jodie came.'

'Jodie?'

'The Snowman. Everybody called him that because of his freaky white hair and eyelashes.'

'Albinism,' Tom said from behind his book.

Faz frowned at the interruption then shrugged. 'That's it. Albinism. Anyway, he was all right at first—he paid off my double bubble for me, read your letters out to me. You know, all that pally-pally stuff. We got along. He was decent.'

'Then what?'

'Then nothing. I got let out early for being a good boy. End of.'

'Don't lie!' Leon growled.

Fazal looked wounded by Leon's tone. 'OK! OK! Frigging heck, Leon. I don't know why you've bothered coming. What's *your* problem?'

'This is.' Quickly, Leon slid the piece of paper his assailant had left him as a souvenir across the table.

Fazal's eyes opened wide as he read the contents. 'It was never that much!'

'What wasn't?'

Leon waited, saw Fazal swallow, look edgy. 'Thing was, right, I promised to pay Jodie back when I got out but . . . I kind of forgot what with getting the new gang together and all that . . . '

'And . . . '

'And then he got out, too, and came round to ask

152

for the money. He didn't believe in double bubble being passed on to the next cellmate. He said it was no way to do business. He gave me an invoice like that one—all neat, all itemized like he worked for Harrods or something. Course, I still didn't take it seriously. I mean, he was just a little fraggle, right? Then it got heavy. Him and his sister started following me round everywhere. Threatening me, threatening my mum. Phone calls in the middle of the night, bricks through the window. Mum was really wound up about it. In the end, I thought I'd try, you know, try to pay a bit of it back but I got caught nicking money from Uncle Raj and . . .'

'I know that part . . . Aayan told me.'

'So I end up back here for violation, dobbed in by my own family. She hasn't been to see me, you know, my mum. Hasn't been once. No phone calls or letters. Nothing.'

Fazal went into a rant, calling his mother foul things he didn't mean but couldn't help. It was either that or cry and no way was that on the agenda. No way. Leon was aware of one of the officers glancing towards them.

'What about the other guy?' Leon asked, keeping his voice low and even.

'What other guy?'

'The Tyson wannabe who busted my ribs.'

Fazal's jaw dropped. 'Leon, I swear on Aayan's life I haven't got a clue.'

Leon stared at his friend and knew he was telling the truth. A buzzer sounded, indicating the end of visiting time. 'I'll bring you some chocolate next time,' he told him.

James waited until he'd seen Tom drop Leon off at the Cropwells' then he walked back into town, had a coffee, and dialled.

Donna answered. He told her he'd been working at the library and wondered if it was OK to drop by for a few minutes until his bus? She said yes, of course. Invited him to stay for dinner. He said yes, of course.

Leon was less delighted to see him but that was too bad. If Leon had problems, he wanted to help. While he accepted Tom had to be around for Emma because of Tia, it didn't mean he could muscle in on the only friend he'd made here as well.

Upstairs, James made Leon repeat everything Fazal had told him. 'So he said he didn't know why this Snowman was after you?'

'No.'

'And you know that's a lie for a start, right?'

Leon shrugged, as James knew he would. 'Let's see this IOU then.'

From between the pages of a cheque book the slip of paper was handed to him. The figure made James's jaw drop. 'That's outrageous! You can't pay this.'

'I know.'

'According to this the double bubble thingy was only half the amount. Where'd the rest come from? What was your friend paying for? Room service?'

154

'Dunno.'

'So how much have you paid already?'

Leon told him. James scowled. 'Idiot! Now they will think you're loaded. Anyway, that's forty per cent off the bill already.' He tapped a figure on the sheet. 'What's this mean? "Expenses"?'

'I don't know, I didn't ask for a breakdown, did I?'

'Well, you should. They're obviously meticulous. Whoever worked all this out pays a lot of attention to detail so you have to. You know what the first thing you have to do is, don't you?'

'What?'

'See Fazal's mother.'

'Why?'

James sighed, shook his head. 'You know what? For a BB gun-toting hoody-wearing black kid with a police record you are incredibly naive sometimes.'

Leon stepped down from the bus on Gregory Boulevard feeling disorientated at first. Then, as he absorbed the sounds and smells of the wide street with its mixture of houses and small shops and fumy traffic, the old familiarity returned and Leon found his heart soaring as he adjusted. He belonged here! He could fit back in just like that! His mood deflated slightly when he took a right up one of the side roads and reached the empty fabric shop above which Mrs Mahmood and her boys lived. The shop was still boarded with wire mesh guards as it had been since Fazal's dad had died, the landlord not having found anyone to take over the lease and Mrs Mahmood, with her boys to look after and being prone to panic attacks, unable to.

Leon paused by the side entrance, noted its broken skylight boarded up with an old wine box. That was new; not that it made much difference to the overall shabby and neglected appearance of the rented house. Nervously, Leon pressed the button for their flat and waited. 'Who is it?' Fazal's mum asked apprehensively. It was Sunday afternoon; she wasn't due any visitors.

'Leon. Please let me in, Mrs Mahmood. It's about Fazal and it's important.'

Maybe it was the shock of knowing he was actually on her doorstep. Maybe it was the knot in his voice that convinced her. Whatever it was, she let him in.

He spent an hour in the flat, feeling claustrophobic. After months of living in Wellington Road, Fazal's harsher living conditions hit him hard today. The sight of the mouse droppings along the skirting boards, the smell of damp seeping from the ancient, peeling woodchip. It was all so . . . sad.

After she had ushered a protesting Aayan and his brother into their bedroom to play, Leon told Mrs Mahmood about Fazal and why he'd stolen money from his Uncle Raj's till and she listened and she believed him. She shook her head in dismay. 'Typical! As if being sent to prison isn't bad enough for him he has to make things worse for us all when he's there, too! Why does he do these things, Leon? When he knows I need him at home? He has shamed this family so many times.'

'It's not all his fault. The rules are different inside. He messed up.'

She sighed. 'He has never been the same since his father died. He turned bad then. Missing school. Lazy. Arrogant. Full of big ideas . . . cheeking me back like they do in *EastEnders*.'

'He's not bad underneath, Mrs M. Not really.'

Fazal's mother looked at Leon. Her eyes were circled by dark rings; she looked washed out, exhausted, an old woman at thirty-five. 'I hope not, for his sake, or next time it won't be just that I don't visit him. I will cut him off, Leon.' She sighed. 'I will see my brother Raj. I will ask him for help—again. I'll put up with that haughty look of derision from my sister-in-law—again. I will tell Raj his nephew is a thief but for a reason. He will be more understanding.'

Leon shifted uneasily in his seat, feeling as if he'd betrayed Fazal, dropped him right in it. When James had told him that he'd already helped Fazal more than enough by giving the Snowman money, he'd seen the sense in that. When he told him these things could go on for ever if they weren't dealt with properly, he'd seen the sense in that. 'Do you like playing the role of the fall guy?' James had asked. No, he didn't. But Fazal was still his best mate and if he needed help, he'd give it. End of.

'When are these people coming?' Mrs Mahmood asked.

'Tomorrow teatime.'

She nodded. 'I will see to it.'

James stayed over that night. He told Leon he wanted to go over the plan but Leon suspected he wanted Donna's home cooking just as much. After dinner, they went into town and chose loads of DVDs from Blockbuster. All, at James's insistence, classic gangster films in order to get into the criminal mentality: *The Godfather* I and II, *Lock, Stock and Two Smoking Barrels*, *Goodfellas*, *Layer Cake*. None of them were what you could call 'feel good' movies. 'Planning a bank robbery then, lads?' Nick asked them when he came in to say goodnight.

'No, but you might want to watch out for that horse's head on your pillow, Mr C,' James quipped.

Nick laughed. 'Night, lads. Switch everything off when you come up.'

Leon didn't see what was so funny. 'It's not a joke, this, you know. These people aren't messing around,' he scolded James when Nick had left.

'Lighten up; it'll be fine,' James replied.

'You try lightening up when your ribs look like this,' Leon said and lifted his T-shirt to show the bruising that had now blossomed across his midriff in glorious technicolour.

'Shit!' James gasped.

'And there'll be more where that came from tomorrow if your "Mr Big" idea goes belly-up. For both of us.'

'Not Mr Big, Mr Hagen,' James corrected, trying to keep his voice from shaking.

Neither of them could get to sleep. 'Maybe I should just go to the bank and get out the rest of my money,' Leon whispered.

'No,' James whispered back. 'Do that and you're screwed, especially as it's not enough. They'll be back again and again.'

'Yeah,' Leon sighed. His eyes followed the arc of a car's lights as it swept across the ceiling.

'They hit you where it hurts most, people like this. They find your Achilles heel. Like Imogen always calling me gayboy to wind me up because of Dad. It really used to get to me until I found out why she did it. Now—nothing. I'm immune. With you, it's money. They've seen you're good for it, so they're coming for it.'

You're wrong, Leon thought. Money wasn't his Achilles heel; he couldn't care less about money. His soft spot was the same as James's and Fazal's. 'My dad . . . ' he said out loud, then stopped abruptly.

James looked across the dark room to Leon's bed. Leon never talked about his father. 'Your dad?' he prompted.

Leon hesitated. This was a big decision for him: telling James about his past. But if the Snowman already knew about his parents—and from the previous conversation it was obvious he did—the guy might bring it up again tomorrow. Maybe try to use it for leverage? To make him blow a fuse? Because winding him up about his parents was one of the few things that could do that. And if he lost it—really lost it—James would be wrong-footed. Disadvantaged because he wouldn't know what the dude was talking about. Maybe even in danger.

Of course, he could be way off-key. The subject might not arise. The girl might be all sweetness and light again. The brother, too, but he couldn't be sure. Had no idea what tactics they might use when they found out he had no intention of paying them any more money. He only knew how vulnerable he was when it came to talking about that time in his life he'd rather keep hidden.

He took a deep breath. 'My parents split up when I was little.'

'Sounds familiar!'

'I lived with my dad; my mum was not around—she liked to party too much. Dad did his best but he used to get low, do you know what I mean? Then, when I was about seven, my mum turned up out of the blue with this new guy, wanting the house back. The solicitors said she was entitled to half so Dad got lower still. He went into a real dark mood; didn't go to work, didn't shave—all that. Then he seemed to pull out of it; he got high, excited, full of ideas. He arranged to meet her privately, to discuss things . . . ' Leon paused, his mind rapidly editing and compressing everything that had happened to the bare minimum. 'Dad picked me up after school in this flash car he'd hired and Mum was already in the front. She was really quiet and her head kept flopping from side to side. When I asked why, Dad just said she was tired. Turned out he'd pumped her full of sleeping tablets.'

'God!'

'Anyway, he drove us to a garage and locked the car door. Set the ignition on . . . you can guess the rest.'

James swallowed. 'They died?'

'Aha.'

'Shit!'

'I would have died too if some kids hadn't found me.'

'What, they smelt the fumes?'

'No! Carbon monoxide's odourless, man. No, they'd seen the car as we drove in and come back to nick it, thinking we'd left.' Leon snorted. That still got to him. That his life had been saved by thieving little twockers. How twisted was that?

'Leon. I don't know what to say.'

'You don't have to say anything and I don't want you to feel sorry for me, right? I'm only telling you in case they use it tomorrow.'

'Let them try,' James said defiantly.

'Yeah. Let them try.'

In the morning, the pair of them set off for college for appearance's sake and returned to Wellington Road as soon as they knew the Cropwells would have left.

They spent the rest of the day watching the DVDs again, each hiding their growing anxiety from the other, their brave words from the night before seeming a little hollow in daylight. James sent Emma a text, telling her he had a stomach bug and wouldn't see her at lunchtime. She returned his message immediately, telling him to get better soon and she'd see him tomorrow. 'Hope so,' he replied, the image of Leon's bruised ribs looming large at that stage.

Late afternoon, the letterbox clattered at the exact time they had been told the letterbox would clatter.

Leon stood up, looking jittery. 'OK,' James told him, straightening the tie he'd borrowed for the occasion with unsteady hands, 'action.'

At the door, Leon heard the letterbox rattle again and saw the flap beginning to open. Not wanting to see those tapeworm fingers again, he flung open the door, startling the woman on the other side who was half standing, half squatting. 'Thanks a lot!' she said, holding her hand to her throat. 'You scared me to death!'

Leon, distracted by her violet eyes and white eyelashes, looked beyond her to the bronze car parked a little way up. 'You can come in,' he told her clumsily.

'Come in?' she asked, puzzled by the invitation.

'Yeah. We, my . . . accountant, Mr Hagen, and me, we'd like to discuss some of the details of the debt with you and the Snowman dude.'

The woman ducked her head so she could see into the Cropwells' hallway. 'I hope this isn't a trick, Leon.'

'No tricks.'

She studied him closely then nodded. 'I'll go get Jodie,' she said.

What happened next was, as James would describe in years to come, bizarre in the extreme. The albino siblings entered the Cropwells' kitchen, shook hands with him and sat down at the table. They were older than James had expected, maybe in their early twenties, tall and striking. Jodie had his hair short and gelled, trendy; the girl (Leanne—he had to ask—it was only polite) wore hers long and tied back. If it hadn't been for their matching dove-white eyebrows and eyelashes, they would have looked as if their hair had been dyed with peroxide, punk style. Other than that, they were just like everybody else, James was disappointed to note. In fact the girl was wearing the same Coast top Emma had, which freaked him out a tiny bit.

Leon made them a drink, as planned. Be polite was number one on the agenda. Leanne requested apple juice. Snowman had tap water. Then they got down to business. 'Leon said you wanted to check something over with us?' Leanne asked him. She tilted her head to one side, looking at him respectfully, willing to listen.

At least she's giving us a chance, he thought. The lisp helped, too—the 'thed' for 'said', the 'thumthing' for 'something'. Made her less moll-like.

He glanced towards Leon, knowing he was relying on him to get him out of this mess, no matter how bizarre it all seemed. Despite feeling totally out of his comfort zone or any other zone for that matter, he knew he had to pull off the bluff of the century for Leon's sake. The guy didn't deserve any of this. He'd been through enough.

James cleared his throat, prepared to put on his best toff's voice that seemed to intimidate people so much. 'Yes, I do have a query or two. I'd like to know which creative chef produced this little soufflé of a number,' he said, tapping the offending digits on the original 'invoice' with his finger.

The pair of them leaned forward, their white heads almost touching, like bouquets of bleached hay. 'Most of that was for hiring Denby,' Leanne replied.

'Denby? What? Pottery?'

'No, Denby—the one with the rings.' She sent Leon a look of remorse.

'You mean the man who assaulted my client?' James asked.

'Yes. Then there was petrol on top.'

James shook his head in a sorrowful manner, just as the real Tom Hagen, Don Corleoni's accountant, would have. 'Regrettably those are not transferable expenses.'

'What do you mean?' Jodie asked. His voice was surprisingly deep.

'Well, with respect, you undertook those, not Leon, or even Fazal.'

'I dunno about that.'

James didn't either but he couldn't back down now. 'Oh, I can assure you it's true. Though the cost may be tax deductible if you're registered as self-employed,' he added, remembering how his mother always seemed to offset the most random things against tax.

Leanne and Jodie exchanged glances. 'No, I thought not,' James continued with growing confidence. 'Now, here's our proposal. Leon has negotiated a settlement with Fazal's uncle . . . '

'What sort of a settlement?' Jodie asked.

James slid the figure across. 'This,' he replied. 'It covers the original er . . . double bubble, less forty per cent my client has already paid, less the cost of repairing the broken window to Mrs Mahmood's property . . . '

'What, he'll pay this? Seriously?' Leanne asked. 'We went to his house and it's a dump. There's no money there.'

James hesitated, not wanting to say yes if it wasn't true. He didn't want to be next on the hit list. He glanced towards Leon for reassurance.

'They'll pay,' Leon mumbled, sliding a flyer from Fazal's uncle's business across to them. 'Go to the address on this and ask for Raj.'

Jodie skimmed the details then said calmly, 'If this turns out to be bogus, we have to come back here; you know that, don't you?'

Leon nodded and glanced across at James whose expression read 'told you'.

Jodie continued, wanting to explain. 'I lent him that money in good faith, you know. I felt sorry for him. Double bubble's a sick rule. He was getting a proper kicking in Briarswood.'

Leon flinched; didn't want to hear it, but Jodie took a sip of water then continued. 'His cocky attitude didn't help. Nobody likes plastic gangsters. Then he got greedy. He started asking me for money for other stuff; non-essentials. He promised he was good for it; said he had things lined up on the outside.'

'Yeah,' Leon sighed, 'sounds familiar.' He loved Fazal but that didn't mean he was blinded to his faults.

Leanne tutted, shaking her head at her brother. 'Jodie's soft like that. Lending people money. Dad goes mental with him.'

'Dad?' James asked.

Jodie shot his sister a warning look. 'You don't want to know. Let's just say Denby works for him sometimes.' He returned to Leon, seeming anxious to make him understand. 'Fazal promised he'd pay me back; swore on his brother's life. That counts for something where I come from. Then when we saw where he lived we thought we'd never get a penny of it so we had to use the surety he gave us.'

'Me,' Leon said with a slight shrug.

James, perturbed by the fleeting but sinister reference to Jodie and Leanne's father, became anxious to end the fiasco as soon as possible and produced his best fountain pen. He unscrewed the top and handed the barrel over to Jodie with a flourish. 'Now, if we're all in agreement and you'd like to sign here . . . here . . . and here to write off the debt . . . ' he said.

Amazingly, Jodie did. 'Pleasure doing business with you, Mr Hagen,' he smiled.

'Or is it James?' Leanne asked mischievously.

'Either will suffice,' James retorted, struggling to keep his composure at being so easily rumbled.

They left then, but not before Jodie had taken their cups over to the sink and Leanne had bent to stroke the sleeping Danziger in her basket. They were the unlikeliest pair of gangsters James could have imagined but he didn't underestimate them for a second.

'Take care now,' they called out as Leon closed the door behind them.

As soon as he heard the car roar away, James went up to Leon and slapped him on his back. 'Well, old son, I've got to say it: "it's been emotional."'

Leon stared back at him, glassy eyed. 'I'm going to take the dog out,' he said.

'Goodness me! Such things!'

'I know. Incredible, isn't it?'

'And they never bothered him again? This Jodie and his sister?'

'Nope. Kept their word. Fazal's mum kept hers and Uncle Raj paid them off. When Fazal came out of Briarswood the second time he was on best behaviour. Butter wouldn't melt.'

Kazia was about to ask something else when there was the sound of footsteps on the corridor outside followed by the low drone of a vacuum cleaner. She sprang back from the exhibition piece and hurried across to her trolley. 'Well, this is all good but now I must definitely get on with my job.'

Hearing the panic in Kazia's voice, Emma dashed over and stared at the array of cloths and cleaning materials. 'Where do I start?' she asked.

Kazia waved a hand airily. 'Oh, leave it, leave it.'

'No, I promised. Come on. What do you want me to do? The sinks?'

Quickly she grabbed a cloth and a bottle of yellow-ish liquid that looked close enough to the stuff they used at home and marched to the double stainless steel sinks in the far corner of the studio.

'Not that cloth!' Kazia said, rushing over and swapping what to Emma looked like one identical checked square for another. 'That is for my tables; this is for my sinks. We cleaners are like artists, too, you know. We like to use certain tools for certain jobs.'

'Sorry,' Emma said, accepting the correct 'tool', her eyes opening in dismay at the state of the sinks. Were they always so dirty? So splattered with paint and clogged up with bits of debris? Globs of newspaper and tiny mounds of plaster adhering, mollusc-like, to every face of the sink's deep sides? She'd need a pneumatic drill to get that lot off!

Meanwhile Kazia escorted her bucket and mop over to Consequences Part Three. This is where she would begin to clean the studio floor tonight, she told herself. Taking the mop, she swished it casually, almost gracefully, backwards and forwards on the floor area directly beneath the montage. She liked this piece, she *decided. He said to her/she said to him. There was so much to see, especially when Emma explained everything. Who would have thought Leon would have had such a story? Amazing! Who knew what else was hidden here, waiting to be revealed. Maybe it wouldn't hurt to read a few more of these caption things, while she mopped, of course.*

A sequence of pictures of Grace caught her eye now. They had been taken in front of what looked like the rubber plants in the canteen. In the first shot, Grace was shown holding a scroll of paper in her hand, in the second she was tearing it in half and in the third she was holding the torn halves aloft, a triumphant grin on her face. What Kazia thought was significant, now that she knew so much, was not the photographic techniques Emma had used but the fact that Grace wasn't wearing her football shirt. She always wore her football shirt! Instead, she had on a tight-fitting cardigan with a stark white T-shirt beneath. How different the girl looked!

Kazia stopped mopping to read the accompanying speech bubble. 'Well, Grace, writing is certainly not your strong point, is it?' it read.

Kazia smiled to herself and tried mopping again but it was no good. She just had to ask. 'Emma . . . '

SHE SAID TO HER . . .

. . . 'Well, Grace, writing is certainly not your strong point, is it?' Mrs Fletcher said with an exasperated sigh.

'Never said it was,' Grace replied.

The tutor flicked over the A4 sheet of paper, scanning the badly structured sentences and the points half made and undeveloped. It pained her to think it but her ten-year-old daughter could have done better. It wasn't as if the girl hadn't been given any help, either. She had received a worksheet with bullet points and key ideas all set out for her. Honestly, the standard of English from these students these days was appalling! 'Do it again,' she told Grace briskly, sliding the sheet across to her.

Grace scowled at the essay but made no attempt to retrieve it. If the woman thought it was so useless she could chuck it in the bin herself or preferably stick it where the sun didn't shine . . .

Mrs Fletcher now turned to Grace's appraisal from her first placement at Jack 'n' Jill's private nursery the previous term. There was slightly better news here. The owner had been pleased with Grace's 'hands on' approach and 'positive relationship' with the children but did mention she sometimes 'resented advice from authority' and her appearance was deemed to be 'over-casual', something she had told her herself. It was high time all these matters were addressed. She folded her neatly manicured fingers into a steeple ready to begin but even now the girl was fiddling with that blasted football shirt! She had the attention span of a gnat. 'Well, Grace, as you know you've got your final placement coming up. This is the big one, where you put everything you've learned so far into practice.'

'I know,' Grace mumbled.

'We've put you with a registered childminder in Balderton . . . '

Grace scowled into her lap. A childminder's? She might have known! That was the lowest of the low, that was. She'd hoped to be in a nursery attached to a school at least. Guess who got those places though? The brainy lot on the diploma course. As if they were any better than her! It was all fixed this; fixed and confirmation of exactly what she had thought all along. Mrs Fletcher had it in for her.

The tutor continued. 'The childminder is called Anita Delaney. Mrs Delaney's very experienced and looks forward to meeting you. She even asked what your favourite biscuits were so she could get some in. That's a good start!'

'Mmm,' Grace agreed, wondering why the name sounded familiar.

'But,' Mrs Fletcher said, reaching out to tap Grace's knee, 'we need to get you a makeover.'

Grace pulled back, startled. 'A what?'

'Clothes send out strong messages.'

'So?'

Mrs Fletcher raised one eyebrow and adjusted her trendy spectacles. 'So basically the ladette look has to go.'

'Why does it?' Grace asked. 'It's dead practical this shirt; if anything gets spilt on it it's easy to wash out.'

'I'm sure it is but that's not the point.'

'What is then?' Grace retorted, folding her arms and pouting which did her no favours with Mrs Fletcher.

'Grace, I'm going to be blunt with you. The only reason you are still in my classes is because you seem to be very good with children.'

'I thought that was the whole point, being good with children?'

'If only! Looking after under-eights means stacks of paperwork—individual care plans, accident reports, letters home to parents, and goodness knows what. Not only that, if you don't know how to fill the forms out properly and accurately in the workplace you can find yourself in deep trouble. They're to safeguard you as much as anything.'

'Huh,' Grace replied unconvinced.

'Do you want to complete the course?' Mrs Fletcher asked coldly.

Grace dropped her arms and her attitude and nodded. Of course she did! She couldn't let her mum and dad down. She couldn't let herself down.

'Then this is what I suggest you do . . . '

'Then this is what I suggest you do,' Grace mimicked in front of Emma and the two lads at lunchtime. 'It's like being back at school.' She pushed her plate of chips away, fed up.

'But did you wear your County shirt to school?' James asked reasonably.

'No.'

'Well then.'

'Well then what?'

'Well then, that proves you are capable of pulling something over your head that isn't in black and white stripes. It won't hurt you to wear a jumper or something instead. I'm with the wicked Mrs F on this one.'

'It doesn't have to be clingy,' Emma added, remembering the incident at Leon's.

'Yeah, right.'

'Look, I'm going into Lincoln on Saturday to buy Tia some new clothes. Why don't you come with me and I'll help look for things with you?' Emma offered.

'Can't. We're at home to Mansfield,' Grace grunted.

'Sunday then.'

'It's not like I'm even in a nursery or a school or anything. I'm just at a childminder's in Balderton,' Grace continued.

'Oh? Which one?'

'Mrs Delaney on Birch Hill Lane.'

'No! That's who Tia's with. Oh, she's lovely.'

Grace rolled her eyes. 'I knew I'd heard the name before.'

'Sunday then?' Emma repeated.

'I suppose.'

'I thought you were seeing me on Sunday?' James complained.

'I'm sure you can live without me for one weekend,' Emma told him.

'I beg to differ.'

'Differ away, James,' she told him, 'this is a girl thing.'

Emma loved shopping for clothes. All her friends agreed she had 'an eye' and they always took her with them if they wanted something special. When choosing, their hand would stray towards an item of clothing on a hanger and then they would turn to Emma for her opinion. Emma would either nod once or shake her head. No words were needed. She had a ninety-nine point nine per cent accuracy rating.

'What's your budget?' Emma asked as soon as she met up with Grace outside the Waterside Centre.

Grace held out the banker's card her mother had handed over to her with far too much enthusiasm that morning. 'Mum says she doesn't care what I spend,' she mumbled.

Emma smiled until her dimples could dimple no further. 'Excellent! Then the only thing against us is time. The shops close at four and it's nearly twelve already. Come on.'

'I need a coffee first,' Grace declared. 'I can't shop without a coffee first.'

Emma frowned. She'd had to promise she'd look after Becky next Saturday to get her parents to have Tia today. Grace had better be taking this seriously. 'One coffee,' she compromised, 'small. To go.'

'I have to sit.'

'What?'

'I have to sit to drink coffee or my kidneys jack in.'

Emma sighed. This was going to be more of a challenge than she had anticipated.

In Starbucks, Grace was the chattiest she'd ever been. Asking about Tia, telling her about the match yesterday, talking ten to the dozen about anything and everything. 'So how's it going with James?' she now asked.

'OK,' Emma replied, tapping the face of her wristwatch in case Grace thought she was fooling her with these lame delaying tactics.

'He's so in love with you, isn't he? You can just tell. He can't take his eyes off you.'

'Mmm.'

Grace tipped a second sachet of brown sugar into her coffee. 'Do you love him?'

Emma felt herself turning scarlet. This wasn't why she was here, to answer awkward questions. The truth was no, she didn't love James. She was fond of him and he was great fun to be with and the physical side was red hot but—and it was a major but—James was also too intense and too needy. 'I like him a lot,' she told Grace, 'but I don't love him.'

'Is that cos you still love Tom?'

Emma almost choked on her coffee. Come right out with it, why don't you, sister! 'No it is not! Now stop trying to distract me and drink up. We're here to buy clothes not talk about my love-life.'

Grace opened her mouth to protest but was interrupted by her 'Three Lions . . . ' ringtone belting out. She scowled when her mother's number flashed on her screen. 'Mam! What?' she asked when she answered it. With an even deeper scowl, she thrust the mobile at Emma. 'She wants to speak to you.'

Emma took the phone, nodded and said, 'How did you guess?' followed by 'yes' and 'oh, really' a lot before she handed the phone back to Grace.

'What did she want?' Grace huffed.

'Come to the toilet with me and I'll tell you.'

Grace screwed her face up. She hated girlie stuff like that. 'Just tell me here.'

Emma drained her coffee. 'Come on,' she urged, nodding in the direction of the Ladies.

In the spacious disabled cubicle, Emma leaned against the hand-dryer and pointed to Grace's backpack. 'Look inside your bag,' she ordered.

'Why?'

'Your mum's put something in there for you.'

'What?' Grace asked suspiciously, sliding the bag from her shoulders and unclipping the fastenings.

'Side pocket beneath your tissues,' Emma directed.

Grace pulled out a pink carrier bag folded several times. Inside was a bra. A pretty, lilac bra. 'I am not wearing that thing!' Grace fumed, stuffing it straight back into the carrier, her face thunderous.

'Why not?' Emma asked, snatching the bra from her to examine it properly.

'It's a mastectomy bra. For women who've had breast cancer. She keeps getting them off the internet for me.'

'I know,' Emma said.

'Well I haven't had breast cancer, have I?'

Emma ignored her—Mrs Healey had warned her she'd say that—marvelling instead at the details on the bra she wouldn't have noticed if Grace's mother hadn't informed her; the openings down the side seams of each cup, masked by lace, to enable the user to slide in either a prosthesis or a shaped cup or whatever the wearer had been recommended. In this instance, the right cup contained a white, lightweight foam enhancer, but the left was like any other cup, waiting to be filled by a breast. 'I think this is so clever,' she said looking up at Grace, a catch in her voice. 'In fact, it's a wicked piece of design work. Fashion at its best; functional and attractive.'

'Is it?' Grace asked uncertainly, glancing at the thing properly for the first time.

'Put it on, Grace, please.' Emma held the bra towards her friend, her eyes pleading silent encouragement. 'Please,' she repeated quietly.

'Don't look then,' Grace muttered.

When Grace swivelled back round, Emma tried pressing her lips together to prevent herself from smiling but the bra fitted so perfectly and she couldn't help it. 'Oh, Grace, it looks really, really lovely. Is it comfy?'

'I suppose,' Grace grudgingly admitted, tugging at the strap.

'Why not leave it on then?' Emma asked casually, her heart beating fast. She knew she had already achieved a miracle—even getting Grace to put the bra on would be that, Grace's mother had told her—but if she agreed to keep it on, well, that really would be something. 'She'll listen to you, Emma,' Mrs Healey had said. 'I might as well be talking to a brick wall.'

Grace glanced down at the twin lilac peaks protruding from her chest. They looked . . . they looked normal, she realized; like those women she had always envied in the lingerie section of catalogues. Nobody could tell she only had one breast. Nobody could tell she was wearing a mastectomy bra even though she hadn't had a mastectomy. And most of all, Emma had said it was fashion at its best—and Emma knew what she was talking about. Grace had never looked at the bras and padded crop tops her mother kept buying like that before. As fashion. As something pretty. But Emma was right: it *was* comfortable and it made her feel . . . different. She took a deep breath, overawed as the peaks rose and fell as she did so. 'Yeah. Well. Might as well keep it on,' she agreed, pulling her long-sleeved T-shirt over the top and her County shirt over the top of that.

During the next three hours, Emma made Grace try

on every item of clothing in Lincoln, or that's how it seemed to Grace. The weirdest thing was, she didn't mind. When Emma said things like 'Brilliant! Perfect! That so suits you,' she believed her. In one shop—Monsoon or River Island, she couldn't remember—Emma told her the purple slash-necked jumper she was wearing looked foxy.

'Foxy?' Grace said, standing back and appraising herself in the mirror for a long time. 'Don't be daft.'

She bought it in two different colours anyway.

Grace arrived in college the next day with a smirk on her face; she couldn't help it. She felt as if she was walking on air. Who would have guessed the difference a half-padded bra and a few new clothes could make? A lad she'd known from school had wolf-whistled as he rode past her on his bike on Bowbridge Road this morning. As for her mam . . . her mam was probably still crying her eyes out as she washed the pots even now. 'You look gorgeous! Gorgeous! Doesn't she, Frank? She looks gorgeous!' she had repeated time and time again at breakfast.

Talk about over the top! In reply her dad had flicked open the newspaper and muttered that his daughter had always looked gorgeous. 'You will still wear your shirt to the match?' he'd asked worriedly. She'd laughed and told him of course she would.

Even Mrs Fletcher complimented her. 'Goodness me, Grace, I almost didn't recognize you!' she said as her eyes swept over her smart tailored trousers and tight fitted shirt. 'Well done, you!'

'Thanks.'

'Now all you need to do is excel on your placement and you should pass the course.'

'Yep. No worries,' Grace replied unfazed by the demand. If there was one thing she could excel at, it was working with kids.

'Aww!' said Kazia, her face a picture of sympathy for Grace staring out at her in her 'foxy' little purple jumper. 'Aww.'

Emma returned her cloth to the trolley and came to stand next to the cleaner. She wiped her hands down her boilersuit but didn't look directly at the picture of Grace. Looked anywhere but, in fact. 'You were a good friend to Grace, Emma,' Kazia continued. 'You helped her. Gave her confidence.'

'I suppose so.'

'And Grace was happy with this Mrs Delaney? She excelled?'

Emma didn't reply but let out a strangled sobbing sound. Kazia turned and was alarmed to see Emma on the verge of tears. 'What is wrong?' she asked. This was all so sudden! Out of nowhere!

Emma could only shake her head. 'Sorry,' she said, embarrassed and upset at the same time, 'it still gets to me.'

'What does?'

180

Emma pointed to a small photograph just beneath the Christmas one then immediately fumbled in her pocket for a tissue. Curious, Kazia leaned towards the picture and then gasped. 'Oh!'

Emma blew her nose hard. 'I know. I know.'

'Maybe you should take this picture down,' Kazia suggested as Emma tried in vain to stem further tears. 'You do not want examiners to see you like this.'

Emma shook her head emphatically. 'No.'

'Why not? If it makes you cry?'

'I'm OK, honestly. It's just going over everything in so much detail with you. It won't be like this tomorrow. It won't be as thorough.' Emma blew again and attempted to smile. 'It had better not be anyway!'

'I have no idea how it will be,' Kazia said with a helpless shrug.

'Well, even if it is, it'll do me good. You have to face your demons in art, right? Like Tracy Emin's "My Bed"? Lay everything bare, no matter how much it opens old wounds.'

Kazia nodded. A photograph of Emin's installation was one of the first things Phil had shown her to illustrate his point about distinguishing between art and garbage. 'You see, you would have changed the sheets and tidied up the mess, Kazia,' he had rightfully pointed out, 'thereby destroying one of Britain's most significant works of the late twentieth century.'

It had been a defining moment in her career as a cleaner of art studios, just as she sensed this picture had been a defining moment in Emma's journey as an

181

artist. 'I understand,' Kazia said, patting Emma's sleeve.
She searched for the speech or thought bubble to
match the picture. 'There are no words for this one?'

'No. No words,' Emma said, swallowing hard, 'the
picture says it all.'

It was midway through Grace's fourth week on her
placement with Anita Delaney and she was loving it!
Her reservations at being placed with a childminder
instead of in a nursery had been totally vanquished.
Anita was great, she'd made her feel really welcome, like
an important part of the set-up not some inconvenient
body foisted upon her. She was good with the kids, too:
patient and kind and fair. The days were flying by.

It was quarter to five and only Tia remained; Anita's
other charges being mornings only on a Wednesday.
Grace was in the playroom with Tia, struggling to get
her arms into her padded jacket for when Emma
arrived any minute to take her home. Tia was having
none of it and was waving her arms and shuffling her
bottom to try to escape in true rebel style. 'Monkey,
you're like a little monkey!' Grace laughed, tickling
Tia's tummy. Tia was just the sweetest baby; she had
huge dark eyes above her round peachy cheeks and
tight curly hair just a shade lighter than Emma's. Grace
adored the baby and Tia adored her.

'She's taken a real shine to you!' Anita had observed,
not realizing that Grace knew Emma and had already
bonded with Tia on other occasions. Not that it would

have made much difference. All babies reacted the same way to Grace.

'Are you laughing at me? Are you? Are you?' Grace cooed, making Tia laugh even more.

The phone started ringing in the hallway and Anita shouted through from the living room for Grace to get it. Grace sighed. Anita was much nearer but of course she wouldn't answer because all she had done for the past two hours was watch TV. 'Here we go again!' she told Tia in a sing-song voice that belied her frustration. 'Multi-multi-tasking!'

Despite Grace's admiration for her, Anita did have one tiny fault: she was addicted to speed auctions on the TV. At first, Grace hadn't taken much notice; she had put the fact that the wide screen TV in the living room was switched on all day, on the same gameshow channel, down to the same reason her gran had hers switched on all day—background noise. Besides, Anita didn't usually actually stop and watch the shows while the kids were around; she waited until they'd left or were having a nap before tuning in to the screen.

Today, though, Anita had been transfixed since lunchtime, entrusting all the childminding to Grace. 'What's the big deal?' Grace asked when an earlier phone call had gone unanswered.

'Oh, it's the best auction they've ever done!' Anita had replied breathlessly. 'A holiday in Australia plus twenty thousand pounds to spend, and look: my name's still flashing at the bottom! If I win that I could go and see our Hannah in Canberra!'

'Good luck then!' Grace had said and left her to it. It was no skin off her nose; she'd rather play with Tia than watch TV any time.

Now there was only fifteen minutes of the auction left and Anita's number still kept flashing up as a potential winner. Every so often Anita would let out a cry of 'yessss' as another contestant bit the dust.

The phone continued to ring. Grace plucked Tia from the floor. 'Come on, Smiler, let's go see who's on the phone.'

Sitting on the edge of James's bed, her face flushed, Emma batted James's hand away as it crept once more inside the blouse she was trying to fasten. 'Hello! Someone trying to be professional here!' she chided James as the phone at Anita Delaney's rang and rang. She frowned. Why wasn't anyone picking up? Come on, come on. It was hard enough she had to call in the first place and fabricate some convincing reason for being late; waiting made it even worse. *I've been working on a sculpture and completely lost track of time,* she rehearsed for when Anita or Grace finally answered . . . *'I'm so, so sorry.'* They'd buy it; they were both so easy-going, so accommodating. It didn't ease the guilt, though, and if her mum found out what she'd been really doing she'd go mental. Having a night on the town with the girls to let your hair down once in a while was OK but skiving classes to be with James because Imogen was away and then missing

184

the bus because you were . . . well, *at it*; that was pushing the boundaries.

Emma glanced round at James, still shirtless, his collarbone jutting as he rested on his elbows, staring at her in the dreamy, far-away-oh-so-in-love look. The artist in her wanted to capture the exact pose, the exact expression in pencil or charcoal. He is adorable, she thought to herself, unable to resist tracing the contour of his collarbone with her finger. 'Why is nobody answering?' she asked.

James shrugged, pulling her close.

'Oh, you can leave Tia with me,' Anita said as Grace walked through the living room towards the phone in the hallway.

'Are you sure?' Grace asked.

Anita's eyes never left the screen. 'Of course! I just don't want to talk to anyone right now. Take a message and tell them I'll call back OK?' Her eyes were bright, her face shining; she was so in the moment but then she unexpectedly held her arms out to take Tia.

Grace hesitated—all her instincts told her not to hand over a baby to someone so inattentive but Anita turned and grabbed Tia anyway, jiggling her up and down on her hip and leaving Grace empty handed. 'Look, Tia,' Anita said pointing to the screen with her mobile phone, 'there's only two names left. Two! Mine and some silly man from Northampton. We don't want him to win, do we? No way!'

Tia waved her arms about in total agreement. 'Ka!'
she said.

Grace headed for the hallway and answered the
phone. 'Hello?'

'Finally!' Emma laughed with relief. 'Listen, Grace,
I . . . ' Her sentence was cut short by a triumphant
yell immediately followed by a sound that made the
hair on her neck bristle and Grace drop the phone.
A half-scream. A heavy thud. Silence. 'What was that?'
Emma cried into the abandoned receiver. 'What was
that?'

Everyone has flashbacks. They come unexpectedly,
making us shudder; those ghostly reminders of an incident we'd rather forget but to which the mind clings
obstinately, no matter how long ago the event, no matter how ancient the memory. Grace's flashback is of
the scene in Anita Delaney's living room that afternoon. The childminder sitting up on the wooden floor,
the scatter rug twisted round her feet, her face ashen
and bewildered. Tia lying so, so still where she had
fallen when Anita's jump for joy at winning made her
lose her footing on the rug and she had slipped and
skidded and fallen, dropping Tia, wrenching her ankle.
Tia hadn't fallen far, just straight to the floor, her head
catching the edge of the marble fireplace. A small, thin
line of blood trickled from Tia's head onto the hearth
and dripped, almost daintily, onto the floor. *She's dead,*
Grace thought, *my friend's baby is dead.*

* * *

Grace cannot remember calling the ambulance but she must have done because two arrived almost at once.

Grace cannot remember having to be prised away from Tia by the paramedics but it must have happened because it was in their report. 'Young woman reluctant to leave infant.'

Grace cannot remember her call to Emma's mobile in a flat, monotone voice telling her to get to the hospital quickly but she must have done because Emma was there, with James, in hysterics.

Grace does remember feeling bereft when she was escorted away from the A and E department where Tia had been rushed, looking so, so small on the trolley, her head and body encased in an ugly cage-like contraption. She remembered biting deep into her lip when she was told she could not wait with the family members, who arrived like something from a DVD on fast forward—blurred but all with that same desperate and grim look on their faces as they passed her in the corridor—Emma's mum and dad with Becky first, then Dan, still in his work clothes, leaving a trail of plaster-powder footprints from his boots. Some time later came Emma's grandma Veronica followed by Tom with his parents.

While all this was happening Grace was called to an anteroom to give a statement. 'Do you want me to come with you?' James asked, needing something to do to distract him.

Grace shook her head. 'Call Leon,' she told him and he nodded.

Anita was just coming out of the anteroom as Grace was being shown in. Her red-rimmed eyes contrasted vividly with her white face as she struggled to use the crutches she'd been given for her twisted ankle. She didn't acknowledge Grace whatsoever which was fine as far as Grace was concerned because she didn't know what she would have said if she had.

A door was opened by a smart looking woman in a suit; her expression kind and reassuring. 'Hello, Grace, I'm Rachael Key, the registrar,' she said, 'come through.'

Beside her in the room was a nurse who smiled the same reassuring smile and bade Grace sit on the chair, its grey prickly fabric still warm from Anita.

Rachael began asking Grace questions. She was unintimidating and patient but Grace couldn't get the words out. Her mind had blanked as soon as she had taken a seat and she mumbled and stumbled through her answers, unable to explain what had happened. The only phrase she did use that rang across the small room was one she kept repeating over and over. 'It was my fault.'

'We're not here to blame anyone,' Rachael was at pains to point out, 'we just need the facts at this stage.' The girl then rambled on about auctions and other things that didn't tally with Mrs Delaney's distressed but still clear, professional explanation at all. 'Are you

188

sure, Grace?' Rachael kept asking as she and the nurse exchanged glances.

'No,' Grace whispered.

In the end Rachael wrote down what she could, telling Grace she should go home and rest. Grace stared at the woman in disbelief. She was going nowhere.

Zombie-like, she joined James and the just-arrived Leon in the reception area of Accident and Emergency. They spoke little to each other, watching vacantly as other dramas were unfolding, unheeded, around them. A mother with her ten-year-old son who threw up a lurid yellow liquid into a metal dish; a harried house-wife with her half-severed finger wrapped in a bag of peas. 'That'll teach me to rush his dinner!' she'd told the nurse on triage before promptly fainting. A down-and-out, shuffling backwards and forwards, sipping from his can of Special Brew and talking to himself.

It was some time after eleven before Emma emerged. She walked towards them slowly, in a daze, clinging to Becky's hand for support. Becky was sobbing and hiccuping at the same time.

Leon and Grace both swivelled round and waited for her to speak but James sprang out of his seat and tried to put his arm round Emma's shoulder; an arm that she shrugged off in an instant. 'Sorry,' he said, trying not to let the gesture hurt him. 'How's Tia? What's happening? Nobody will tell us anything because we're not family.'

Emma took a deep breath in as she prepared to say

out loud the incredible, tongue-searing words. 'They think . . . they think my baby's got a fractured skull,' she blurted out.

'Oh, Emma,' was all James could think of to say.

'That means she could be brain damaged!' Emma glanced over his shoulder towards Grace but their eyes darted away from each other like aeroplanes avoiding a mid air collision. Instead she leaned close to James and whispered in his ear, 'It's all my fault; if I hadn't been with you . . .'

'Don't say that!' James protested, his heart hammering painfully in his chest. Before the phone call—that gut-wrenching phone call—he'd been thinking life couldn't be more perfect. He had few enough precious memories; he didn't want this one taken away from him. Please. 'Emma,' he began but he was interrupted when Tom appeared. 'Erm, Emma, the doctor's here,' he called, his voice strained, scared.

James, distressed by what Emma had said, tried to follow but Leon, observing everything from a distance, was already pulling him back, holding him close in a bear hug. 'Come on, mate. This isn't your gig. Back off.'

And James knew he was right; knew he had no place in this family crisis and that cut him deeper still.

At one o'clock Steve, Emma's father, emerged with Becky. He managed a smile for the three friends, surprised and impressed they were still around. 'Hey,' he said, stopping briefly by their chairs.

'Hey,' James replied, 'any more news?'

Steve nodded. 'Well, it's not as bad as they first thought. Tia's got a lateral fracture of the skull but as skull fractures go it's the best one to get: the least dangerous and the quickest to mend.'

James felt relief sweep through him. Relief for Tia's sake. Relief for Emma's. 'Thank God.'

'She'll be in for a couple of days for observation and as long as she doesn't fall asleep for longer than normal or show any other symptoms, she should be as good as new . . . '

'That's great news,' James whispered.

'Yeah, man,' Leon added.

Steve glanced towards Grace, who had dropped her head and was sobbing quietly into her hands. 'Accidents happen, Grace,' he said and patted her trembling shoulder as he left.

By three o'clock, Leon and James had fallen into an uneasy asleep across each other but Grace remained upright, rigid and pale, reverting to staring at the posters, her face scratchy and dry from crying. Now, instead of seeing Tia lying on the living room floor when she closed her eyes, all she could think of was Emma not even looking at her when she'd come in, then whispering in James's ear. She had asked James what she'd said, wondering why he'd cried out 'Don't say that!' so piteously but he'd just looked sheepish and said 'nothing'. Nothing? She didn't believe that for a second; he was just trying to be kind. She knew what Emma had said. *Look at her sitting there when it's all her fault! What a nerve! Can't you get rid of her?* She bet she had said that; something like that anyway.

Grace began to nibble the edge of her nail, barely noticing she was tearing and gnawing the skin. She didn't see her parents come in; was unaware of them as they approached her warily, exchanging nervous glances when they saw how gaunt she looked. Aileen slid her ample body on the spare chair beside her daughter and pulled her gently towards her and started stroking her hair. 'Come on, duck, let's get you home,' she whispered.

Grace tried to shrug her off but she was too exhausted to resist for long and allowed herself to be led out, almost in a trance. 'Either of you two lads want a lift anywhere?' Frank asked Leon and James.

Leon accepted immediately and James's shoulders sagged in submission as he glanced towards the eerily quiet corridor, knowing with chilly certainty that Emma wouldn't show. As he followed the foursome into the cold night air, he couldn't help wishing he had a mother with such no-nonsense arms as Mrs Healey's to cuddle him and take him home.

Grace woke early the next morning, automatically got dressed then remembered what had happened. The memory winded her and she collapsed on the edge of her bed with a sharp sob. Slowly, she began to get undressed again, undoing her cardigan and her shirt and letting them drop to the floor. Then she unclipped her bra and discarded it. From her bottom drawer she pulled out a washed-out grey crop top. From the drawer above, she found her County shirt and pulled that on over the crop top, feeling swamped and safe, custard over apple pie, gravy over chips, just like the old days.

A few minutes later, her dad found her sitting high on her bed, cross-legged, her duvet round her shoulders, looking for all the world—in his own words—'like an old Red Indian squaw'. 'I've brought you a cup of tea, duck,' he told her, placing the steaming mug next to her alarm clock.

'Thanks,' she mumbled.

'The hospital phoned.'

'Yeah?'

He cleared his throat, trying not to convey any anxiety. 'They've had to refer the incident to social services. Cos of the circumstances, like. There seems to be a bit of difference between what you said and what Mrs Delaney said and what with Tia being a baby and that . . . '

'Just tell them it was my fault. That's all they need to know, isn't it?' Grace muttered, hugging the quilt even closer.

Tia was discharged three days later, as sunny as ever and totally unaware of the fall-out around her. Emma refused to leave her side, watching over her every millisecond of the day. Tom was granted some time off university and came over to help as much as he could. 'This just arrived,' Tom announced, bringing a huge helium balloon tied with bright yellow and pink ribbon into the kitchen. 'Welcome home, Tia' was emblazoned on either side of the balloon.

Emma barely glanced at it and continued to coax Tia to finish her lunch. 'Put it with the other stuff over there,' she said dully.

'It's from James.'

'Mmm.'

Tom set the balloon among the vases full of flowers and the presents that had already arrived.

'Have you called him back yet?' Tom asked.

'What? Who?'

'James. Put the poor sod out of his misery! He's left endless messages.'

Emma sighed impatiently. 'I haven't had time.'

'You would have if you let me do something!'

'Meaning?'

Tom came to sit on the other side of the table, where Tia was fastened securely into her booster seat, making a right royal mess of her lunch as she revelled in smearing macaroni cheese everywhere. 'I could help feed Tia, for instance.'

'I can do it.'

'So can I. Come on, Em, have a break. Go into town. Meet James for a coffee or something. You heard what the consultant said: Tia's fine. She needs to be treated as normal. We need to act normally around her.'

'I'm feeding her homemade macaroni cheese and carrots. What's abnormal about that?' Emma snapped.

Later, when Tia was having an afternoon sleep, Tom tried again. 'How about I drive you down to college later? You could pick up some coursework?'

Emma shrugged and began clearing away the lunch things. 'No need. I talked to Phil this morning and told him I was dropping the course.'

Tom stared at her in disbelief. 'But why? It doesn't make sense.'

'Looking after my own baby doesn't make sense? How'd you work that one out?'

'But you don't have to pack in college! Tia's fine and you know my mum's offered to pay for a full-time nanny. One who'll come to the house . . . '

'Forget it,' Emma stated firmly. 'Looking after Tia's my job from now on not some stranger's.'

'But jacking in college? That's a bit OTT, isn't it?'

Emma glowered at him, irritated that he didn't seem to understand. 'Look, the only way I'd go back is if you shared the responsibility like you said you would that time? You have her during the day while I have her at night.'

Tom paled as he struggled to reply. No way could he give up his course, his other life.

'No,' Emma said, her voice scathing as she slammed the dishwasher door shut, 'that's what I thought.'

* * *

Two weeks after the accident, a letter arrived for Grace from social services giving the date for the hearing. Frank, arriving on his doorstep from a long stint on nights at the same time as the postman, opened it without Grace's knowledge and shook his head in sorrow. He quickly folded the letter in half and tucked it in his back pocket. 'Right then, duck,' he asked Grace cheerily, 'what are we having for breakfast? Your mam got some of that lovely bacon you like from Porter's. Do you want me to make you a butty before I get to bed?'

Grace pulled the quilt round her shoulders and poured hot water onto her tea bag, watching it bob on the surface like a square lifebelt. 'No thanks, Dad,' she mumbled, 'I'll just have this.'

'Go on!' he encouraged. 'Get a bit of fat on your bones.'

But Grace had already made her tea and drifted upstairs again, where she planned to spend the rest of the day, as usual, in bed.

Frank Healey gazed at the open doorway then re-read the letter. They'd make mincemeat of Grace the state she was in right now. The poor lass's career would be over before it had begun and that would be a tragedy, that would. Bad enough she'd already told Mrs Fletcher she was not coming back to college, even though Mrs Fletcher had said her place was open for her, without making matters worse for herself by admitting to something she hadn't done. No way had their Gracie dropped that baby. No way on earth.

Rubbing his hand tiredly over his bristly chin, Frank checked his watch and grabbed his car keys. 'Just popping down to your mam's shop for some milk,' he called upstairs.

No one answered.

At break, James did a double-take at the two people sitting in the sofa area next to Leon. He didn't recognize the woman but the man looked just like Grace's dad. As he neared and realized it was indeed Mr Healey, his consternation grew. 'Hi, Mr Healey. Everything OK?'

Frank half rose then sat back down again. 'Not bad, James, not bad. Er . . . do you know Mrs Fletcher? Grace's childcare tutor . . . as was.'

James glanced towards the woman and nodded. 'No, but I've heard a lot about you,' he said, sending Leon a sidelong glance.

'Mrs Fletcher's very kindly agreed to put in a word about our Grace at the hearing and . . . '

'What hearing?'

Mr Healey quickly explained.

'Oh,' James said. 'Is that why Grace hasn't been around? We've been wondering where she was. Tried her mobile a few times but nada.'

'No . . . er . . . she's been a bit under the weather lately.'

'Yeah, I know the feeling,' James sighed, staring into his coffee. 'Has she spoken to Emma?'

'No.'

'No, me neither. I guess she'll be in touch with us all when she's over the shock of everything.' *Said he, living in ever decreasing hope, James added to himself.*

'Trouble is we haven't time. Grace won't call her and me and Aileen can't, so I thought you might be able to tell Mrs Fletcher instead.'

'About what?'

'What you told me that night in the car. About hearing the scream.'

James visibly flinched. The sound, and the immediate events after it, were things he wanted to forget, not re-live. But if it helped. He cleared his throat. 'Emma had just . . . Emma had just missed the bus so she phoned to tell Mrs Delaney she'd be late . . . '

Nearby, Leon listened as James filled in the details, wondering if it would be possible to have one week at college, just one week, where nothing weird or dramatic happened.

Julia Fletcher waited for the door to open, feeling apprehensive. She was so out of order being here, yet she also knew it was the right thing to do. Moments later a shadow appeared behind the frosted glass and then the door opened, revealing a pale Anita Delaney, leaning against one crutch. She didn't seem too surprised at seeing her. 'You'd better come in,' Anita sniffed.

She led the tutor to the kitchen and offered her a coffee. 'It's from a flask, I'm afraid. I still can't get to and fro so well. The bruising's still coming out.'

'That's fine,' Julia soothed, glancing over her

shoulder towards the living room. 'No . . . er . . . children today?'

'I'm not fit enough yet,' Anita pointed out.

'Of course. I'm sorry.' Julia cleared her throat. 'Anita, I was wondering if I could clear up one or two points with you . . . for my college records. You know what it's like after an accident—miles and miles of red tape . . . ' Julia knew she had to begin tentatively. As well as a duty of care towards her students she also had a duty of care towards the people who volunteered to take on her students. She had to tread carefully and not make hasty judgements, no matter how moved she was by Frank Healey's pleas on his daughter's behalf.

The childminder took a deep breath. She still seemed shaken by the whole thing. 'Where do you want me to start?' she asked.

'From when the phone rang?'

There was another, more juddering intake of breath. 'I was upstairs in the bathroom when I heard the phone. Next thing I heard this awful scream and I ran downstairs, saw what had happened . . . but I was so anxious to get to Tia I went skidding on the rug and went over on my ankle. Talk about making matters worse!'

'But you do know you should never have left Grace alone with the baby? She should have been supervised at all times?' Julia pointed out.

'Of course I know,' Anita whispered. 'I've accepted full responsibility for that in my report. I just hope people will understand that even childminders have to answer a call of nature now and again!' That was it; the much-rehearsed line she was going to use at the hearing. It sounded plausible enough, said out loud.

Julia took her canister of saccharin from her handbag and tapped one into her coffee thoughtfully. The fact that Anita had so readily acknowledged her responsibility would stand in her favour as would the fact that Grace had admitted culpability. And yet there was something about Anita's tone that didn't ring true. She decided to probe a little. 'Well, thank you, Anita. I can write all that up for the college report. They still need the facts, even though Grace has left college.'

'Has she? That's a shame,' Anita said, aware she needed to be careful.

'It is a shame; she had potential but I think she feels so guilty about everything.'

'I know how she feels. Like I said at the hospital, if I hadn't been upstairs it would never have happened . . . '

Julia leaned forward conspiratorially. 'Well, between you and me, it's not just about the accident. Apparently, Grace was good friends with Miss Oji and the loss of the friendship is hitting her as hard, if not harder, than the accident.'

'Are they friends? Oh. I never knew that,' Anita replied.

'Oh yes. She was the one who was on the end of the line when Grace took the call.'

Anita's eyes widened as the implication sank in. 'I hadn't realized. How strange . . . I . . . '

200

'Aha. And apparently she heard some sort of jubilant cry that Grace put down to you winning some speed auction thing? Her boyfriend James was there as well. He heard it too. He'll be at the hearing, I think . . . ' Julia Fletcher let the information dangle like damp washing on a line and was rewarded with the sight of Anita Delaney's face changing to a coarse, unearthly grey.

After Julia Fletcher had left, the childminder stared into the distance, her world collapsing around her like a sandcastle engulfed by the incoming tide. What had she been thinking? The crazy, panicky thoughts of an addict, that's what. Stupid, stupid, stupid. Of course she was never going to get away with blaming Grace. Even if the tribunal believed her story about being upstairs at the time, the fact that she'd won the trip to Australia was bound to come out sooner or later. Then what would they think?

Anita shook her head. The most stupid thing of all was that it was Grace who'd given her the idea. Going on about it being her fault as they'd ridden to the hospital together in that second ambulance. Well, she had thought, seeing a glimmer of hope for retaining her reputation, if she *wants* to take the blame . . .

In the living room that evening, Frank Healey replaced the telephone receiver and turned to his wife with a look of relief and joy on his face.

'Well? What did she say?' Aileen demanded.

Frank blinked, his eyes having gone all watery for some reason. 'Job's a good 'un,' he said. 'The woman's admitted it. Changed her statement and everything.'

'Goodness gracious! Such things!' Kazia gushed. 'That must have been a horrible time for Grace but especially for you.'

'Tell me about it!' Emma shuddered. She bent towards the photograph of Tia, the one she had taken, perversely enough, while Tia was being rushed on a trolley through to A&E, her head engulfed in that horrible cage thing. She had taken it just in case it was the last one she had of Tia while she was still alive. And afterwards she had not deleted the shot, looking at the chilling image over and over again to remind herself what a bad, bad mother she was, or at least thought she was at the time.

'But Tia is fully recovered?'

'Oh, yes, totally. She's nearly three now. Look, here she is.' Emma walked across to her bag and pulled out the same camera, flicking back through a series of recent stills of Tia about to go to a birthday party dressed up as a golden fairy.

'Adorable!'

'Well . . . mostly!' Emma agreed, a proud expression on her face. 'She can be a little diva. I have no idea where she gets that from!'

Kazia made the sign of the cross on her chest.

'Thank God she is better. And everything turned out all right with everybody? With Grace and James? I know you said you gave up college course but you went back to canteen and sit together, sometimes?'

Emma sighed and slumped her shoulders. 'No. I never went back.'

'But you saw James again? And Leon and Grace?'

'I didn't see Leon for a long time. He stayed on for a second year at Hercules Clay so I bumped into him in town a few times. James left the minute he finished his last exam that May. I never saw him again.'

'Never?' Kazia asked in astonishment.

'A few weeks after Tia came out of hospital I sent him a text telling him it was over.' Emma chewed her lip. She couldn't believe she'd done that to him. It was such a harsh way to end it. Unfair. 'I wasn't thinking straight for a long time. Dan said I was like an extra from Shaun of the Dead; in a trance, like I'd been hypnotized. In fact it wasn't until Mrs Giannakopoulos phoned me out of the blue during the summer holidays I snapped out of it.'

'Mrs Giannakopoulos?'

'Darius's mother. Darius; the little boy Grace used to babysit for?'

'Oh yes. The Bad Burglar!'

'Well, she called me one day, really apologetically, saying it was none of her business but could I possibly find it in my heart to forgive Grace because she was such a good babysitter and Darius missed her so much. Of course, I didn't know what she was talking about! "Well, you know," she said, "since Tia's accident. I know it must have been awful for you but it's been awful for Grace, too. She won't go near children now; her confidence had been so dented. So if you could call her . . . "'

Emma paused, looking at Kazia with large, round eyes. 'I hadn't a clue about any of this! Even the tribunal stuff. Mum had dealt with all that, thinking I had enough to contend with.'

'Sure. It makes sense she would do this.'

'Anyway, I went round to Grace's house with Tia, and talk about a reality check. Grace looked dreadful! I don't think she'd brushed her hair for months and she certainly hadn't washed her daft football shirt. It reeked! I think seeing her in such a state snapped me out of mine. The worst bit was when I went to give her a hug and she flinched; I think she thought I was going to thump her or something. That really shocked me.'

'Yes. It is understandable.'

'So, long story short, we had a talk; cried buckets, got through about fifty boxes of tissues . . . '

'Poor Grace. Poor you!' Kazia sympathized. 'And now?'

'Now we're fine; really good friends. We've come full circle.'

'Especially you, Emma, because you are back here? At Hercules Clay? That is full circle?'

'I guess so.'

'What made you come back? Was it Grace?'

'No. Not really. I made the decision myself. I stayed

home with Tia for a year and then a few things happened. Once the whole zombie-in-a-fog thing cleared and I realized Tia actually was better and wasn't going to sink into a coma any second I became restless. I loved Tia but I missed my art and I missed mixing with people my own age. Trouble was I still felt uncomfortable about leaving her with anyone outside the family so I didn't know what to do. Then fate intervened.'

'Fate?'

'Yep. You know, when everything just drops into place for once? At the end of what would have been my second year, Grace finished her first year at Hercules Clay that she had retaken and was offered an assistant's post in the college crèche. How perfect was that! If there was one person outside the family I would trust with Tia it was Grace. I went in to see Phil and ask if I could resume my course and because I'd done so much in my first year and had new stuff I'd done at home, he was happy to take me back. I put Tia down for a place at the crèche and got her in. So now I have the best of both worlds. I drop Tia off with Grace, head upstairs here, knowing I'm two minutes away if Tia needs me. Sorted!'

'Aw!' Kazia said, her eyes brimming with sentimental tears. Without thinking, she wrapped her arms round Emma and gave her a warm embrace, kissing her on both cheeks as she would any of her nieces or nephews in Wroclaw. 'I can go home now with big smile on my face.'

'Oh! But don't you want to see my last piece?' Emma asked.

'Last piece?'

Emma pulled Kazia alongside her. 'Yes! The icing on the cake, baby! Kazia, I present to you, at long last, and in reward for your commendable patience and wonderful input, Consequences Part Four: The Consequence Was.'

Kazia frowned. The panel Emma had led her across to was blank. Just a bare stretch of white nothingness. 'The Consequence Was?'

Emma smiled. 'You know your piece of paper?'

Kazia nodded. She knew her piece of paper. It was here in her pocket. She took it out and showed it to Emma, who read it out loud.

'Boy's name Dan; Girl's name Meredith; Where they met: A & E department; He said to her: You have nice eyes, Doctor Meredith; She said to him: I am just thinking same about you, Danny boy.'

'I did those last two lines when I was cleaning Phil's office!' Kazia confessed.

Emma laughed. 'That's ace, Kazia. You really are a legend. Well, the final thing you write, in Consequences, is the consequence, or outcome,' she explained.

'I see that. I accept that,' Kazia said, returning to the bare panel, 'but I am still not understanding how this is the consequence. The end. There is nothing here.'

'Press the buttons.'

'The buttons?'

'The white buttons on the bottom.'

Sure enough, on closer inspection, Kazia noticed three

white buttons, as well camouflaged as polar bears on snow, arranged along the bottom edge of the panel. 'I just press?' she asked.

'You just press,' Emma smiled.

'Any?'

'Any.'

'Then I go for this one,' she said and jabbed at the first button on the left. Immediately a man's voice echoed round the studio and a film began. Kazia's jaw dropped. The panel was a TV screen. How clever.

'I think I need to adjust the volume on that,' Emma said nervously but Kazia wasn't listening. She was glued.

THE CONSEQUENCE WAS . . .

The young man on the screen was sitting in front of a long window, his back leaning against the wooden shutters, his legs raised on the recessed seat. Kazia let out a small cry. It was James, but he had changed so much from the photographs in Part Three. So much broader! So handsome! Then he began to speak, straight into the camera, eyes shining. 'Hi, Emma! James here. Of course I'll help you with your art project. Wouldn't want you having to complete it all by yourself now, would we? Not having a dig at you or anything but, I mean, where were you when I was sitting my physics A2 paper last week? Nowhere to be seen, as per.'

'Get on with it, you pillock,' a voice hissed.

'Who is that?' Kazia asked.

'Quinny. He's doing the filming. He stayed on a third year to try again for Oxford.'

'They are back at school?'

'Yes.'

'St Jerome's?'

'Yes.'

'When was this taken?'

'Last month . . .'

'So this is what James looks like now? Today?'

'Yes!' Emma said, her voice almost disappearing. It had shocked her, when she had watched the film for the first time. She had not seen James since the hospital waiting room. What shocked her most, two years on, was not how James had changed but how her stomach had fluttered as she had watched. As it was doing again now.

'He is very good looking boy.'

'Man. He's nineteen now. He's a man.'

'Good looking man.'

'Shh! Kazia; you're missing half the film!'

Kazia glanced at Emma's profile, saw the rapt expression on her face and smiled. She looked just like Meredith when she gets in the lift with married but handsome Doctor Shepherd and did not expect to see him there. She is acting cool but feeling hot. 'OK,' she said, 'I watch.'

'Neat idea, by the way, Oji: Consequences. I like it,' James continued, 'not too arty-farty but with just enough of the old deep and meaningful. Examiners love that stuff! Hello, examiner! OK, so you want me to just say a few words on the consequences of my stupendous GCSE results; the ones I took the first time around in the days of yore. The ones I deliberately failed for a bet. Well, I suppose now I'm older and wiser and taking psychology A level, I'd better start by saying I don't think I failed them for a bet at all. I think I did it just to see how Mother Dearest would react. I was testing her *lurve*, as any decent quack will tell you. Having tested it and found it wanting, I was made to come to terms with the fact that basically, I had a crap family. I mean, I saw Mum like twice that year, even when Immy was half-starving me.'

James paused and looked thoughtful, then shrugged. 'But I'm not going to go all Dave Pelzer about it; I mean, there are plenty worse off than me. Look at how Leon coped, right?

'Course, things changed once Mumsy discovered I had been re-taking my GCSEs again all along and not doing hairdressing. Her face that August when I delivered my super-duper string of A stars in contrast to the previous occasion . . . priceless. I was back at Jerome's quicker than you can say Chippendale chair. All that family stuff aside though, failing my GCSEs did have one positive outcome. I met you and that, pathetically but honestly, is still the best thing that has happened to me.'

'Aw, sweet!' said Quinny.

James showed him his middle finger but Kazia could see James was faltering now, his gaze less steady at the camera. He seemed distracted, like an actor in dress rehearsal who had forgotten his lines and needed prompting. 'Um . . . what else? I learned to appreciate the value of education? Does that sound worthy enough? I . . . um . . . learned every action has a reaction . . . oh, scratch that, I'm back to physics again. OK, *c'est le fin*, Quin.' James's eyes darted briefly back to camera. 'That's it then, Emma. Good luck. And if you see Grace or Leon say hello to them for me. I've been totally abysmal at staying in touch. And love to Tia, of course, and regards to Tommy Boy, if he's still around. Um . . . call me if you ever fancy a chat . . . '

James studied the camera for a moment as if about to say something else, then looked away, jumped down from the windowsill and disappeared from view. 'Right then, Quinny, I'm parched; let's go for a pint,' he said off-camera.

The film ended.

'Oh,' said Kazia.
'Move on,' replied Emma quickly.
Kazia nodded and pressed the second button.

Grace appeared. She was sitting on a small red plastic chair, peering into the camera. Over her clothes she had a polo shirt with a little rainbow motif Kazia recognized as the uniform belonging to the college crèche. Behind her was a wall display of nursery rhymes bordered by an alphabet frieze. Humpty Dumpty's head rose behind Grace's, making her look as if she were wearing an oversized flesh-coloured bonnet. 'Start then,' somebody prompted.

Grace's eyes flew open. 'Oh! Is it on?'
'Dur!'

'Who is that talking?' Kazia whispered.
'I don't know,' Emma whispered back, *'one of the nursery assistants she works with, I suppose.'*

Grace wriggled on her chair then sat upright. 'Er . . . right then, Emma. You wanted me to make a short film about the consequences of coming to Hercules Clay or something.'

'The impact of your GCSE results,' the nameless voice and film editor prompted.

'Yeah. Whatever. Well, I suppose if I hadn't got a D and an E I would never have got in and I right wanted to do the course but in another way they were bad because if I had failed or got higher grades I'd never have ended up with that Delaney woman.'

Grace paused to tug at her bra strap. 'On the other hand, if all that hadn't happened—not that I'm saying I wanted Tia to fracture her skull cos I'm not—but if it hadn't and I hadn't stressed out and packed in the course then I wouldn't have found out that just because you make mistakes it doesn't mean you're rubbish. You've just got to learn how not to make the same mistake again. What I did was I started my year all over again, only this time I tried a thousand times harder with the essays and Mrs Fletcher helped me tons more this time, mainly because I let her . . . '

Grace stopped talking just long enough to pull her long hair back into her ponytail then addressed the camera once more. She cleared her throat. 'Mind you, Emma, if you hadn't brought Tia round to ours that day, I'd never have gone back, no matter what Mrs Fletcher had said. I couldn't believe it when you told me you felt guilty about Tia just as much as I did. I thought you hated me! Funny, isn't it, how you can get hold of the wrong end of the stick? And that's all I've got to say, really,' Grace summarized, drawing her eyebrows close together. 'Er . . . Emma, you're not going to show this to like thousands of people, are you? I don't want everybody staring when they see me in the canteen.'

'Wave goodbye or something then,' the camera-woman suggested.

Grace waved stiffly and the film ended.

'That is so nice. I am pleased she went back,' Kazia smiled. She was pleased. This was good ending, so far. She liked it very much. Almost better than Grey's Anatomy. *'And Grace is wearing nice clothes again I think?' she added.*

'Oh yes,' Emma smiled, 'there's no stopping her now and she's got a hospital appointment soon about her implant which means she'll soon be able to wear ordinary bras. That is so going to be a red letter day.

213

I've told her she should have a party and flash her new boobs off.'

'Ah yes. Her Poland's Syndrome not from Poland. Well, I am so pleased for her,' Kazia said, her attention back on the screen. 'Leon now,' she correctly predicted and pressed the third button.

Leon did not appear on the screen, only his voice could be heard from behind the camera as he guided the viewer round the interior of a building with a high, dusty red-brick wall broken up by two equally high, industrial-type iron-framed windows set into it, filmy with dirt and cobwebs. In one corner there were two mattresses, covered with duvets and pillows, suitcases stacked at the foot of each.

From there the camera panned to a deep green sofa, tobacco coloured foam protruding from the arms like smoke from a steam train. Opposite, a small portable television stood on a flimsy-looking three-legged coffee table. 'This is my crib in Nottingham. I live upstairs and work downstairs,' Leon began, 'what do you think? Cool or what? The whole building used to be a lace-making factory but now half of it is a furniture warehouse—that's where I work—and the upstairs is like this. I only discovered this bit last week when my boss asked me to bring some empty boxes up. I couldn't believe the waste of space, man, especially as me and Fazal were paying the earth for this nasty little flat in Lenton. So I asked if I could live here and he said

214

sure. It's better for him having people on the premises at night, know what I mean? And he isn't charging anything because Faz and me are going to do all the building work ourselves. I know it looks a bit of a state now but just wait a few months; it'll be mint. Hey, check this out!'

The camera zoomed in on a large pine headboard resting against a far wall, carved into which was an intricate pattern of swirls and sweeping plumes flowing in and out of two co-joined initials. 'I made that for a guy in West Bridgford; he's giving it to his daughter as a wedding present. My skills are in demand! Not bad for a looked-after kid, eh? That is one thing I am grateful for; being sent on that Cabinet Making Course. Mr Marriott taught me well.'

The picture wobbled for a second, went dark, as if blinking, then returned, this time with a panoramic view of the skyline through the window. 'Look at this city,' Leon said, his voice more animated than Emma had ever heard it. 'Isn't it something? See, I don't have a family but I do have a city and it's called Nottingham. OK, I accept that I threw away my last couple of years at secondary school here; me and Faz both did. I guess I had to leave and come back again to find that out.'

Leon fell silent and led the camera across other imposing Victorian buildings, church spires and office blocks, shopping complexes and the hulking arches of the railway station.

'I'm not going to do this job for ever, either. I know Mr Marriott thought I was some genius woodcarver

215

and that's how I got this gig but I'm not really. I just put all my spare time in on my pieces because I didn't have anything else to do so I looked like I had talent but really it was just down to hard graft. No disrespect to him—like I said, he taught me well—but I was biding my time. Faz was off the scene and though the Cropwells were fine people and James was a cool guy, Newark was always only temporary for me.

'So, I don't know about Consequences, Emma, but that time in the lift? The consequence of you having faith in me that day—when you said "He needs friends in college, not prison"—that blew my mind, that did. You doing that, after what I done to you—that's what I'll remember about that period of my life more than anything. It's partly why I'm going back to college. Yep you heard me right! I'm a man with a plan. Going to start with those GCSEs I never took. Then I'm going to get a job working with kids like me and Faz—kids who need a bit of a push in the right direction. Social work or something. Maybe I can help them, you know? So, anyway. Yeah . . . that's it really.'

There was a final shot of the skyline then the recording ended.

'Mmm,' Kazia said, her voice tinged with disappointment, 'I am not sure about that film. I would like to have seen his face. And he didn't talk about the Snowman.'

Emma was incredulous. 'Kazia! I'm guessing that's the most Leon's ever spoken in his life! Why would he talk about the Snowman? It's over, forgotten. I thought showing us his new flat was much more revealing.'

'Revealed he needs me to go clean for him.'

'I'll tell him that. I'm sure he'll take you up on the offer.'

'You will tell him? You still see him?'

'Now and then.'

'So you see Grace and Leon but not James?'

A shadow flickered across Emma's face. 'That's about it.'

'And Tom? You see Tom?'

Emma raised her eyebrows. 'I'll always see Tom; he's part of the furniture! He's at the house now with Tia.'

'Ah yes, you said.'

'He's celebrating his 2:1 by taking Tia to Center Parcs tomorrow.'

'Ah! That is good.'

'Yeah, they'll have a great time.'

'You are not going, too?'

'Hell no. Two's company; three's a crowd.'

'Excuse me?'

'Tom's got a girlfriend now: Victoria. She's twenty-four and has a masters degree in biochemistry or something. Super brainy.'

'Goodness.'

'It's great for Tia because Vicky has a little boy called Caleb to torture—I mean play with!'

'Oh, I see. Tom has . . . um . . . moved on.'

'Big time. I think they might get married; he's well smitten.'

Kazia wasn't sure how she felt about this. She would have liked Tom and Emma to be a couple. That is how it was supposed to be when you had a baby together. But then she shrugged. She knew this is not how real life worked for this generation. 'OK,' she said over-brightly, 'I see your film now, Emma.'

She turned to press the button and frowned. Where was the fourth button? 'Your knob has dropped off?' she asked.

Emma laughed out loud. 'No, my knob has not dropped off!'

'But where is your film? The Consequence Was?'

'I don't need a film,' Emma said, her face radiant, 'this is it! This is the consequence for me.' Her arms swept over each panel at a time. 'Don't you see? My art says all I have to say.'

'Oh. Of course!' Kazia nodded as understanding dawned. Smiling, she searched her pocket for her piece of paper. There was not much space left on which to write. 'So, I just have to give my consequence, yes?'

'Oh, I'd love it if you did.'

'So,' Kazia said, leaning on the bench behind her. 'The consequence was . . . they all lived happily ever after,' she said, reading each word out loud as she wrote. 'This is best consequence of all, no?' she asked.

'Definitely,' Emma agreed.

Kazia proffered her hand for Emma to shake, just as Emma had done at the beginning. Emma took

218

it, shaking her hand warmly. 'Well, it has been good to meet you, Emma. I hope you come top of class tomorrow!'

'Thank you,' Emma replied. She looked at the woman who just a couple of hours ago had been one of the college cleaners, someone she recognized by sight but that was about it. Now Kazia was . . . what? Friend was too strong a word but she definitely felt she had bonded with the woman and was reluctant for it all to end now, so abruptly. 'What did you say you were doing tomorrow, Kazia?'

'During day? I will be shopping then in afternoon cleaning grandfather's grave. Then in evening back here, as usual.'

'I'm free in the afternoon. May I come to the grave with you? I can tell you what the examiners said then.'

Kazia looked delighted. 'Sure.'

Emma grinned. 'See you tomorrow afternoon then!'

Kazia nodded and headed for the stockroom to put her trolley away for the night. At the doorway she paused and turned, smiling to herself as she saw Emma reach towards 'Consequences Four: the Consequence Was' and push the first button.

AUTHOR'S NOTES

- Hercules Clay (died *c*.1644–5). Although there is no college called Hercules Clay College in Newark, Hercules Clay certainly existed. He was an alderman of the town and lived in a house on the corner of the market place. During the Civil War, when Newark was being besieged by Cromwell's parliamentary forces, Hercules Clay dreamed for three nights in a row that his house was going to be destroyed by fire. So convinced was he of this, the next night he moved his family to a nearby dwelling for safekeeping. No sooner had he done so than his house was indeed destroyed by Cromwell's men. To show his gratitude for his narrow escape, he bequeathed £100 to the poor of the town. The money was used to provide poor children with penny loaves on March 11th.

- GCSE stands for General Certificate in Secondary Education. At the time of writing, these exams are taken by pupils in Year Eleven throughout England and Wales. A measure of a school's success is how many of its students gain the higher A to C passes.

As the percentage has increased, the media has derided the results as being worthless and GCSEs as being too easy. How disheartening for the thousands of pupils who work so hard only to be told that what they have achieved is rubbish anyway!

- Tuffee is a regional term for sweets or candy.

- Fraggle: prison slang for a weak inmate, a victim.

- Sweatbox: prison slang for prison van used to transport prisoners.

- *Grey's Anatomy*: US hospital-based drama very popular in our house!

- Poland's Syndrome: a rare condition that is evident at birth. The condition is generally recognized by the absence of chest wall muscles on one side of the body. Named after a British physician, Sir Alfred Poland who first described the chest wall anomaly in his documented observations of the cadaver of a murderer in 1841.

ACKNOWLEDGEMENTS

I'd like to thank Polly and Katharine for loving the idea and Liz for steering me through the wood so I could describe the trees. I'd also like to thank Anne Cassidy for all her support and sage advice.

Many other people helped me along the way with the research for this book. I'd like to thank the staff at Newark and Sherwood College, especially Liz Addington.

I also want to thank the svelte Sarah Bartholomew for putting me in touch with Polly Wainwright and Candy Turton down at the Youth Offenders Team HQ. Polly and Candy were brilliant at helping me develop Leon's storyline as was Steve of the 'Last Chance Project' based at Glen Parva Youth Offenders Institute. Sincere thanks also go to Lynn Farmer from the Poland Syndrome Support Group and Catherine Johnson for helping me with the tricky subject of race and colour.

Helena Pielichaty

Helena Pielichaty (pronounced Pierre-li-hatty) was born in Stockholm, Sweden but most of her childhood was spent in Yorkshire. Her English teacher wrote of her in Year Nine that she produced 'lively and quite sound work but she must be careful not to let the liveliness go too far'. Following this advice, Helena never took her liveliness further south than East Grinstead, where she began her career as a teacher. She didn't begin writing until she was 32. Since then, Helena has written many books for Oxford University Press. She lives in Nottinghamshire with her husband and two children.

www.helena-pielichaty.com

Helena Pielichaty

SATURDAY GIRL

ISBN 978-0-19-275511-7

SWEEPING UP OTHER PEOPLE'S HAIR EVERY SATURDAY IS NOT SUZANNE'S IDEA OF FUN. BUT HER JOB IN THE SALON MEANS THAT SHE CAN HAVE SOME MONEY, SO GIVING UP HALF HER WEEKEND IS A SMALL PRICE TO PAY. BUT DISASTER STRIKES ON THE VERY FIRST DAY . . . KARENNA!

SHE'S ONLY THE JUNIOR STYLIST BUT FROM THE WAY SHE FLOUNCES AROUND, ANYONE WOULD THINK SHE RAN THE PLACE. SHE'S ALSO THE ONE PERSON FROM SUZANNE'S PAST THAT SHE HOPED SHE'D NEVER SEE AGAIN.

SHOULD SUZANNE QUIT HER JOB? RUN AWAY? STAND ON THE ROOF OF HER DAD'S VAN MAKING LIKE A ROCK STAR? OR FACE UP TO KARENNA ONCE AND FOR ALL . . .